"D...

The stranger's face screwed into a grimace with those words as once again pain wracked his body. "Meeting him will only put your life in danger. I'm not going to let that happen. I'm willing to lose it all, even the memories. I can't die like this, with you looking at me as if I were a stranger, Rachel."

He knew her name.

Though his pain had to be excruciating, he struggled to reach toward her. As soon as Rachel understood that he meant to touch her, she backed away, but it was too late.

She felt his touch, a ghostly caress of air against her cheek. Fleeting and eerily cold as it was, she felt a burning awareness.

Then he began to disappear.

Helen R. Myers, a collector of two- and four-legged strays, lives deep in the Piney Woods of East Texas. She cites cello music and bonsai gardening as favorite pastimes, and still edits in her sleep—an accident learned while writing her first book. A bestselling author of diverse themes and foci, she is a three-time RITA nominee, winning for *Navarrone* in 1993.

NIGHT MIST

HELEN R. MYERS

Silhouette Books

Published by Silhouette Books

America's Publisher of Contemporary Romance

SILHOUETTE BOOKS

ISBN 0-373-51127-2

NIGHT MIST

This edition published by arrangement with Harlequin Books S.A.

® and TM are trademarks of Harlequin Books S.A., used under license.
Trademarks indicated with ® are registered in the United States Patent
and Trademark Office, the Canadian Trade Marks Office and in other
countries.

Visit Silhouette at www.eHarlequin.com

Printed in U.S.A.

CHAPTER ONE

Stepping out into the night, Rachel quickly turned her back on the darkness and slipped her key into the door's mortise lock to secure Nooton's Medical-Surgical Clinic for another day. For four hours and twenty-some-odd minutes, to be more accurate. Until Sammy arrived at six in the morning for his ten-hour shift.

A demanding schedule, she thought again. As demanding a schedule as any she'd been subjected to since earning the right to call herself Dr. Gentry. Not that she really minded. After all, it wasn't as though she had someplace else to be. Usually. Tonight, however, was different. That's why she'd been compelled to close early.

But as though to challenge her, the lock refused to budge. Disgruntled, Rachel set down her medical bag and used both hands and a few whispered expletives, determined to offset the effect the Louisiana humidity had on everything in this middle-of-nowhere town. There were, of course, more practical solutions. For instance, she could get the can of petroleum-based lubricant Sammy kept in the janitorial closet. But she'd already lost too much precious time arguing with Cleo and didn't think she could afford to risk any more.

"Come *on*, you stubborn..."

Finally, reluctantly, something inside the cylinder yielded and the key slid all the way to the locked position with a rusty, grating sound that cut into the night's melancholy drone of tree frogs and other, less identifiable nocturnal creatures. Beneath her doctor's jacket her skin tingled the way it used to during those mystery and horror movies her college roommate had insisted on watching after their late-night study sessions.

More aware of her solitude than ever, she wondered again if maybe she'd been wrong not to confide in Cleo. Her senior night nurse hadn't approved of closing early. What's more, instead of explaining, Rachel had simply reassured her that, despite their other nurse being on vacation, there wasn't anything happening tonight. No one would get into trouble for this, she'd added, and Cleo had seemed okay—until Rachel turned down the offer of a ride home.

"You plan to do *what?*" the nurse had snapped, her hands fisted on her size-eighteen hips. "A woman's got no business walking around here at this hour, especially not somebody who don't yet know who's who and what's what around here. Why, you got them oil trucks speeding back and forth from the rigs. You got folks coming out of the lounge hardly able to stand, let alone drive. And we ain't gonna get into discussing the kind of trash that's been known to jump off one of the freight trains rambling through town. Just what're you up to, anyway?"

Rachel had assured her that she simply felt the need for some fresh air, which the walk would provide. Cleo hadn't bought the story for a second.

"This is on account I couldn't drive you on Monday and Tuesday, ain't it? I knew it. You've been acting weird ever since. Trying to make me feel guilty."

It hadn't been easy convincing Cleo that she wasn't trying to do anything of the kind; nevertheless, Rachel had held firm to her decision to get herself home her own way. Suspicious and openly offended, the older woman had sped away with a burst of spinning tires and spitting gravel, leaving Rachel to finish turning off all but the security lights.

It was just as well, Rachel decided, drawing the key out of the door. She picked up her bag and squared her shoulders. Right now she had too many questions of her own without having to answer someone else's.

Come on, Gentry, she cajoled as she found herself hesitating. *You know the plan, and it's too late to turn chicken now. Move. If nothing happens this time, no one need ever know besides you. If something does…well, how much stranger could things get?*

Either way she would be safe in her bed in another twenty minutes or so. Safe, although not necessarily asleep. She sighed, not relishing the prospect of lying wide awake for the rest of the night analyzing what she'd seen and what it meant, while mice, or who knew what, scurried around within her bedroom walls.

Well, don't forget you came down here because you also wanted some adventure in your life, remember?

What a thing to remember. Cleo was right; Rachel had been foolish to insist on walking alone at this hour, even though the boardinghouse stood just across Black Water Creek Bridge. And to do it repeatedly? She had to be tempting fate. How she wished she still had her car; having that sleek curve of steel and fiberglass wrapped around her would be a comfort right about now.

On the other hand, how could she regret selling her parents' graduation gift? She'd accepted it under duress, anyway, and selling it had cut in half the balance she owed on her medical school loans.

Stop wasting precious time, Gentry. Make the one-eighty.

She executed a quick pivot, and her heartbeat accelerated to a stronger thump against her ribs. She forgot about Cleo, the red sports car, even that her feet and back were killing her. She simply stared at the veil of gray obliterating the night sky, along with almost everything else, and knew her instinct to experiment one more time was going to yield results. Exactly what kind, she didn't know, but there would be something.

Mist…as it had for the first two unforgettable nights of the week, once again it hung in the air, consumed it. Bone-dampening, vision-blurring, spring mist. Fog. Floating rain.

Before Monday, she wouldn't have given the soggy weather much thought beyond the fact that it made everything in the boardinghouse smell like moldy bread or overripe cheese, caused her clothes to stick to her body as though they were a decayed layer of skin, and made hard-to-curl hair like hers borderline frizzy. Droll musings. Trivial reflections. But Monday had changed everything, as had Tuesday—and she was losing her ability to remain dispassionate.

She drew a slow, calming breath and reminded herself that she couldn't afford to get too caught up in the atmosphere. She was a doctor. Maybe she had a lot to learn, as Sammy had pointed out, but that didn't mean she shouldn't approach this with logical, methodical and, above all, scientific thinking.

This time she wouldn't overreact. This time she wouldn't make any mistakes. *This* time she would determine what was happening on the single-lane bridge linking one side of the rural community to the other. Oh, yes, she would. Even if it meant being drawn deeper into what was beginning to feel like a bad dream.

With a death grip on her medical bag, and her hand already damp from nerves and the fine moisture hanging in the air, Rachel pocketed her keys, then switched the bag to her right hand. Rubbing her left palm against the side of her jean-clad thigh, she started walking.

As she eyed the spans on the cantilever bridge, illuminated by the lights from Alma's Country Cookin' on the near side and Beauchamp's Gas and Body Works on the far side, an eighteen-wheeler rumbled by. It prompted her to accelerate her pace. If the driver saw anything while crossing, she reasoned, surely he would stop.

But she had just stepped onto the single-lane bridge when she heard the change of tone signifying tire rubber meeting solid ground. The truck had reached the other side and was speeding away. Obviously, the driver hadn't seen anything unusual at all.

No Dr. Watson award for you, old girl.

Somewhere in the distance a bloodhound bayed. Beneath her, bullfrogs croaked their night songs in somber bass, and the indolent creek flowed with barely a murmur. She'd heard it would take several days of heavy rains and severe flooding north of Baton Rouge to rouse this swarthy stream, but mid-July wasn't exactly monsoon season in Nooton, and

in the few weeks since she'd moved here the rain they
did have had been light.

She swatted at a mosquito and then two more, deciding a gully washer would be welcome if it rid them
of at least a percentage of the pesky bloodsuckers.
She'd heard that when they got bad this high up on
the bridge, you knew the population was at epidemic
proportions. Local trivia fact number eighteen, she
thought, making a conscious effort to keep her growing tension in check.

At least her long-sleeved jacket protected her arms,
and her jeans saved her legs from all but the most
persistent insects. But how appalled her mother would
be if she could see her. "No self-respecting Gentry
woman would allow herself to be caught wearing
such attire in public," she would say, her aristocratic
nose angled to insinuate just the right amount of disdain. Well, none of her "genteel" relations would be
caught dead in Nooton, anyway, and they certainly
would never have given up two years of their lives to
fulfill anything as archaic and austere as a two-year
"moral commitment contract."

Almost halfway across the bridge the mist grew
thicker. It swirled as warmer air rose from the creek
and mossy banks to merge with slightly cooler air
currents. Rachel narrowed her eyes, searching each
shifting mass. Her heartbeat raced faster, until it
seemed one constant thrumming. Was that something? Was *that?* The phantomlike mist played trick
after trick with her vision, making her feel as though
she was part of some middleworld and had to wrestle
for control of her imagination.

Oh, God, what was she doing? With another
twenty-two months on her contract, what right did she

have to go on some wild-goose chase that took her attention away from caring for those who relied on her? Suppose an emergency arose and Sammy learned she hadn't been there to handle things as she should have? How would she explain? What person in their right mind would accept the flimsy excuse that she'd been following a theory—one based on mathematics to be sure, but still weak?

"Help me."

She jerked to a halt, the rubber soles of her jogging shoes squeaking against the cement sidewalk, and just as abruptly, all doubts and concerns vanished from her mind. Peering through the writhing mist to the other side of the bridge, she saw it. *Him.*

So, this wasn't a fluke after all, she thought with a contradictory sense of satisfaction and trepidation. He was back, as he had been on Monday and again yesterday.

She studied the vision that initially had made her doubt her overtired eyes. A moment later she heard it again—the desperate words which had been haunting every waking and sleeping hour since she'd first heard them.

"Help...me."

As before, the hairs at her nape and on her arms lifted. Nevertheless, she slowly, cautiously started toward him.

He stood in the darkness and fog, visible only because of his white T-shirt, yet blending in as a result of it. The same man from the other nights, but it struck Rachel that there was something different about him tonight, and it took her several more seconds to realize what it was. He was *standing.*

Amazing. Impossible. On the first night she had

come upon him lying sprawled on the narrow sidewalk, his back braced against steel girders, his long
legs stretched out onto the pavement. The moment
she'd reached his side, he'd expelled his last breath
and vanished into the mist, leaving her stunned, horrified, and concluding she was on the fringe of some
kind of breakdown. Yesterday's experience had been
much the same—except that it had lasted longer
somehow. Neither episode had made any sense.

And tonight he stood. Actually, he was leaning
back against a steel truss. As before, his hands were
wrapped around his middle. But what made this moment equally tragic, or perhaps even more so, was
that this time the terrible flow of blood seeping from
between his fingers had only begun.

"It's me." She cleared her throat, disgusted with
herself because she thought her voice sounded unsure
and shaky. "Please don't disappear. I think I know
the drill now. I'm not supposed to touch you, right?"

"Rachel."

She almost dropped her bag, nearly lost all courage
and ran. Her name was the last thing she'd been expecting to hear. How did he know it?

"Who are you?" she forced out.

"Rachel..."

The agony and concern in his voice tore at her
heart, even as his use of her name unnerved her. No,
she decided firmly, he had to be delirious and was
confusing her with someone else called Rachel. But
his pain-glazed eyes focused on *her,* and his expression, his entire being, reflected that of a man who
knew the end was near...a man who wanted to go
while gazing at the one thing he valued most in life.
But how could that be?

"Ah...jeez. It hurts, Bright Eyes. Hurts bad."

The endearment had her insides doing an unfamiliar flip-flop; nevertheless, she didn't let it intrude on her determination to help—and to get more of her questions answered. "I know it does. I'm a doctor. Maybe I can—"

"Don't touch!" he warned, anxiety overriding his pain. But the expenditure of energy proved costly and he began sliding to the ground. "Just...don't touch."

Barely holding back a cry of despair, Rachel followed him down, landing hard on her knees. She set her bag beside her. "All right, all right! I won't touch." But it meant restraining everything she was, everything she had trained to be, particularly when he looked so tormented. "Look, if you can feel pain, there has to be something I can do."

"Do...yes. I know...I know you have to get out of here, Rachel. If they find out you know me, I think they might..."

"*Who?* What are you talking about?"

Instead of answering, he screwed his face into a tight grimace as once again pain racked his body. Rachel bit hard on her lower lip. Stomach wounds were ugly business, and his challenged her resolve to honor his request.

"Please," she said, leaning as close as she dared without risking accidental contact. "Help me to understand this?"

"N-not sure I get it myself."

"At least tell me your name?"

This time he was the one who looked shocked. "You don't...?" He swore. "Joe. Joe Becket. Say it, Bright Eyes. I need to hear you say it...one more time."

He sounded so desperate, Rachel never considered refusing him. "Joe," she whispered. But his aggrieved expression told her that he knew the name meant nothing to her.

A sound broke from his lips. It may have been an attempt at a bitter laugh, but it sounded more like a sob. "You're not getting it at all, are you? Listen...I've figured out this much. You can't go back."

"Back where?"

"Leave. Tonight. Now. You can't... I can't let you meet... *Damn.*"

"Who? Meet who, Joe?"

"No good. It'll only put your own life in danger. I'm not going to let that happen, understand? I'm willing...willing to lose it all, the memory of you...of us, if it means..."

"Hush now." He wasn't making any sense, and he was using up precious strength. "Try to lie still. Let me think."

He rocked his head back and forth. "No. Won't go like this. Not with you looking at me as though I was some stranger." The pain had to be excruciating, yet he struggled to sit up. Then he reached for her. "Once more. I have to just once more...."

As soon as she understood what he meant to do, Rachel tried to back away from him. But it was too late.

She felt his touch, a ghostly caress of air against her cheek. Fleeting and eerily cold as it was, it left her feeling a burning awareness she knew she didn't dare examine too closely.

Then he began to disappear.

CHAPTER TWO

"No!" Rachel lurched forward—to do what, she didn't know since on some level she understood that any action she took would be pointless—and as expected, he vanished before her eyes.

She balanced herself by resting her palms on the cement, felt something warm and wet, and inspected her hands. They were smeared with blood. Real blood. Closing her hands into fists, she searched through the mist swirling around her. "I don't understand this! Do you hear me? *I don't understand.*"

As if in reply, Rachel found herself illuminated by a pair of fast-approaching, blinding lights. Through the din of a roaring engine a horn blasted her. Certain the wide-bodied beast was broad enough to sweep her up in its path, she spun around and pressed herself flat against the steel beams where Joe Becket had reclined only moments ago.

The eighteen-wheeler raced by. Although it didn't come close enough to hurt her, she decided it had added enough impact to the moment to shock a decade or two off her lifespan.

With her heart thudding in her throat, chest and head, she gulped for air. *Brilliant place to catch your breath, Gentry,* she chastised herself. *Keep it up and you'll become a ghost yourself.*

It was the first time she'd admitted to herself what she might be dealing with, and the thought had her shaking her head in instant rejection. She was a sen-

sible, logical person, she reminded herself, an edu-
cated professional. She'd never had cause to believe
in the possibility, let alone the plausibility, of such
things in all her twenty-nine years. Even while she'd
been gauging the chances of succeeding in this encounter, she hadn't allowed herself to put a label on
it. Him.

Then she inspected her hands. To reassure herself,
since she'd never heard anything about ghosts bleeding. Only, the blood was gone. Except for a few
grains of street grit stuck to her skin, her palms and
the pads of each finger were clean.

"Who are you?" Rachel murmured, staring at her
hands before gazing up into the night. "Who *are*
you?"

She didn't get a reply. At least he was going back
to being consistent, she thought, grasping at whatever
seed of sanity she could. But he did have a name. It
was a start, she decided, pushing herself to her feet
and collecting her bag.

For the rest of the crossing she found herself constantly looking over her shoulder, torn between wishing she would see him again and being relieved when
he didn't reappear. Recurring visions of some past
tragedy were one thing—if that was indeed what she
was dealing with, and it was the one explanation that
made the most sense at this point—but being warned
that she could be in danger put a flaw in that theory,
didn't it?

How had he learned her name? And what about the
intimate way he'd spoken to her? *Bright Eyes.* She'd
received enough compliments about her brown eyes
to accept that people thought they were her best fea-
ture. She'd attributed that to having a fast, inquisitive

mind and a clear conscience. Right now, however, she was less than enthralled with her fascination for pursuing mysteries.

As she walked, she struggled to recall if and when she might have met Joe Becket, but try as she might, it proved useless. They were complete strangers, no doubt about it. With his lean, hard face and probing eyes, he wasn't a man a woman would be apt to forget; her own reaction to him—and she'd been known as a bookworm through school—proved that. Yet she'd done more than notice this injured, brooding being; she'd let him get inside her head...and now she didn't know if she could get him out.

But at the same time, she couldn't miss the irony in that. What safer way to avoid dealing with real human beings, and her sexuality, than by focusing on someone, or rather some*thing,* that vaporized the instant she got close to it? Her mother, who for years had assumed the role of relentless matchmaker, would probably find the situation completely understandable.

No, her phantom was nothing like the smooth-talking, power-hungry men who'd moved in her family's social circle, or even the financially or intellectually aggressive ones she'd met through her own studies and work. There was a harder edge to him; she'd seen it in his deep-set, piercing eyes and in the sharp planes of his face. He seemed the sort you wouldn't relish having as an enemy, and when muted by his sensitive, vulnerable side...well, anyone would find him intriguing.

Not that she couldn't handle it, she thought, giving herself a mental shake. She stepped off the end of the bridge onto the rocky shoulder of the road.

"Oh!" She gasped, landing awkwardly on the uneven ground. Pain shot through her right ankle. In the next instant she was rattled by a splash as something jumped or fell into the creek, which was followed by vicious barking not far downstream.

Spooked, she rubbed at the pain, and, assuring herself that the leg would take her weight, set off again. All she wanted was to get to her room.

Still, her step was more cautious this time as she made a left down the dirt road that ran behind Beauchamp's and parallel to the creek. The meandering path ran through some of the lowest-lying property in the area, and the farther down she went, the denser the fog grew. It increased Rachel's awareness of her solitude and her unease with the dank, dark aura of her surroundings.

When she'd first arrived in Nooton several weeks ago, she'd thought this portion of town evoked an atmosphere perfect for the set of a horror film, the kind with a cast of no less than three dozen corpses. The idea had ceased to be amusing.

Someone obviously *had* committed a murder here. Joe Becket seemed to be proof of that. She couldn't figure out what else was going on, but that part seemed devastatingly clear. The question was, when had it happened? Who had done it? And why? Her thoughts flowed one after the other like the lonely toll of a church bell.

Mrs. Levieux's boardinghouse rose out of the fog. Three stories tall, it was a gothic-style dwelling nestled within a giant's grasp of ancient oak trees. The fog muted the effects of the peeling paint, but at the same time turned it tombstone-white, emphasizing the starkness of the numerous windows. They seemed to stare at her like the hollowed eyes of a skull. Lifeless yet watchful eyes.

Rachel shivered. For all she knew, Joe Becket's killer could be renting a room in there, as she did. As she squinted to see each black rectangle through the mist, she focused on the side of the house, specifically the one at the top floor on the far right corner. Her neighbor's room. The reclusive Mr. Barnes.

If anyone deserved to be a prime suspect, he was the man. No one knew anything about him except that he worked at Beauchamp's and avoided speaking to anyone if he could help it. He wasn't a Nooton native, either. In fact, Mrs. Levieux—Adorabella—had made a point of telling her more than once how he'd moved to town not long before she did.

The pale chintz curtains framing the screened window shifted slightly. Rachel sucked in a quick breath, then reminded herself that after what she'd been through, it was perfectly understandable for her to get a little paranoid—but unnecessary. As eccentric as her neighbor seemed to be, there was nothing going on up there except the night air stirring the curtains. A quick scan of her own window proved hers were fluttering, too.

She was about to turn onto the sidewalk when her gaze was drawn back to her neighbor's window. At that instant she saw the tiny dot of reddish-orange. It grew brighter, and then dimmed…like the burning tip of a cigarette, she concluded, with renewed unease.

Mr. Barnes smoked. Sometimes, when she walked in the hall, she smelled it, and at other times, as well, like when she was in the bathroom they shared. Which meant…?

That was him up there watching her.

For the second time that night, the hairs at her nape and on her arms lifted, radioing messages of fear. What was he doing awake at this hour? From the darkness of the room, it didn't look as though he was trying to watch TV or read.

Maybe he'd seen what had happened on the bridge. She glanced back and decided otherwise; the mist was too thick. But then what was he doing standing there in the dark?

Whatever the reason, Rachel told herself, she didn't need to stand down here and blatantly advertise that she'd spotted him. Ducking her head, she walked briskly the rest of the way to the front steps. It took supreme effort not to break into a frantic run. But at the door, she needed a moment to lean back against the wall, and press her hand against her heaving chest.

Coincidence. That's all it was. There could be any number of innocent explanations. The man probably suffered from insomnia. What with their stuffy rooms and the lack of air-conditioning, why shouldn't he seek the coolest spot—the window?

Even so, she regretted not having asked Mrs. Levieux more questions about him when she'd learned the two of them would be the only tenants on the third floor. Recalling the casual comments—"such a quiet man" and "so private"—which her landlady had volunteered during her initial tour of the house, Rachel now found them oblique and hardly reassuring.

If she sought out Adorabella tomorrow and made a point of bringing him up in conversation, could the old woman tell her more? *Would* she? It hardly seemed likely—not if she hadn't seen fit to share the news about the murder on the bridge. No, the wily old fox had kept silent—probably for the sake of gaining another boarder.

Listen to yourself. You've practically got the poor soul tried and convicted along with your neighbor.

This proved she needed to calm down and figure things out, she thought, digging her keys from her pocket. She opened the screen door and unlocked the glass-and-wood one behind it.

Once inside, she gingerly set the bolt. The extra care wasn't necessary, since there was no great threat of rousing Adorabella. Although the woman normally ran the house like a dowager queen, keeping track of everything and everyone in her tiny kingdom, Rachel suspected that at night a burglar could carry off the antique cast-iron stove in the parlor without waking her. She attributed that to Adorabella's affection for her "medicinal" peach liqueur and an equally potent stash of sleeping pills obtained from who knew where.

But that didn't mean Jewel's antenna was shut down, even if her room was farther back in the house. Adorabella's housekeeper, cook and confidante made the lady of the house look like an innocent. Deciding there were enough watchful souls around here as it was, Rachel proceeded with caution, tiptoeing as she began climbing the first flight of stairs.

There were eight bedrooms on the top two floors of the house, and only four were currently occupied, two on the second level and two on the third. Every night since taking a room here, Rachel had felt it both a blessing and a curse that hers was on the top floor; however, at the moment, all she remembered were the negatives—like how with almost every step the stairs creaked, and how so far she'd managed to avoid only a percentage of them.

When she reached her floor, she paused. Her room was at the end of the hall, opposite Mr. Barnes's. She had chosen it because she'd wanted the view of the creek rather than the barn at the other end of the house, or the woods out back. She'd assumed—perhaps too naively—that Mr. Barnes had chosen his for similar reasons.

The most she'd ever seen of her neighbor was his back as he slipped into his room after using their shared bathroom, or the top of his dark head when he hurried down the stairs. To be fair, there were logical explanations for their lack of contact. Their work schedules were complete opposites. That didn't exactly enhance their chances for striking up a conversation. But fairness wasn't an issue at the moment; her sanity, if not her safety, was.

Suppose he decided it was time they did meet? What if he challenged her the moment she tried to reach the sanctuary of her room? Who could she rely on for help? Mr. Bernard, the retired railroad conductor on the floor below? The poor soul was practically deaf, and Celia Nichols, the sloe-eyed divorcée who had her eye on her boss, the married owner of the Black Water Creek Lounge, spent most of her time over there.

Don't be a fool. The man has never bothered you, and he's done nothing to suggest anything will change.

She was overtired and stressed, that's all. Her job kept her steeped in responsibility. And she couldn't forget the added pressure brought on by her alienated relationship with her family. Even without the burden of the past three nights, she had a lot taxing her mind.

It would do her a world of good to try to let go of everything—including this last episode on the bridge—and start fresh in the morning. She doubted she would get much sleep, but simply relaxing might help. In the morning she would consider confiding in Sammy. He was, after all, her sponsor, advisor and friend, as well as her boss. Most important, he had more background in psychiatry than anyone between here and Baton Rouge; as real as the episode on the bridge had seemed, it wouldn't hurt to make certain she wasn't fabricating the whole thing in her mind due to emotional overload.

But even with her new resolve, Rachel was cautious as she circled the balustrade and entered the bathroom. In fact, she found herself holding her breath until she set the lock.

She placed her bag on the side of the tub and faced her reflection in the mirror, wincing at what she saw. It was worse than she'd expected, worse than when she used to pull marathon shifts as an intern. Her eyes were bloodshot and rimmed in red, as though she'd been crying, and her face appeared as pale as a cadaver. Her dark brown hair, her personal vanity point, was no longer styled in a sleek pageboy cut, but rather a frizzy tangle. Add to it that her jeans and lab coat were stained with who-knew-what she'd picked up from crawling around on all fours on the bridge, and she was a visual horror herself.

A shower would be heavenly, but it could wait until morning when she knew she would be alone on the floor. Instead, she settled for a quick scrub of her hands and face.

When she was done, she leaned over to retrieve the jacket she'd laid beside her bag. At that moment she heard the doorknob twist.

Jerking upright, she inadvertently knocked her bag into the tub and several items fell out.

"Damn it, are you still in there?" a familiar voice growled.

"Yes, but...but I'm almost..."

"I need in. *Now*."

Strange, Rachel thought. Five minutes ago, the prospect of having to face the man had filled her with dread. Indignation, however, provided a blissful swell of courage.

She released the lock and swung the door open, her first impulse being to tell the impolite jerk what she thought of bullies, not to mention voyeurs. Then she met the piercing dark eyes that the light revealed were midnight-blue, stared at the face that was etched forever in her memory and felt the room spin like a child's top gone haywire.

"Hell, lady, whatever you do, don't faint, because I'm in no mood to play gentleman."

His voice, but without the aching tenderness. *His* face, once again grim with pain—but also with frustration and resentment. Joe Becket, but a Joe Becket who was very much the flesh and blood of this world.

What was going on?

"I need to use the sink," he continued, holding up his wrapped left hand. "This has started bleeding again."

Seeing the blood on the thin, filthy rag saved her. Whatever doubts Rachel had about her ability to cope as a woman, or as a specter's medium, they were insignificant in the face of a medical emergency.

Drawing herself straight, she reached for his injured limb.

"Let me see."

He jerked back. "I can take care of it myself. It needs to be rinsed off, that's all."

"From the amount of blood soaked through that unsanitary rag, I think it's going to need substantially more. I'm a doctor," she added when he simply glared at her.

"I know who you are."

Rachel wasn't sure whether it was the fact that he could be so blatant about spying on her or that he was rudeness incarnate and a disappointment; whichever, it prompted her to lift an eyebrow and affect a cool hauteur that was poles apart from the wariness and tension she actually felt. "Then you have the advantage, Mr....?"

She wanted him to say it. She already knew what she was going to hear and that it was already compounding the mystery she'd let herself get caught up in, but she wanted the words to come from his own lips.

"Barnes," he ground out. "Jay Barnes."

CHAPTER THREE

Rachel stared, certain she'd misunderstood. When she'd first opened the door, she'd been shocked. She was just as shocked by not hearing him say, "Joe Becket." Of course, if he *had* said it, it would have made things more bizarre and creepy than they already were. But it would also have given her the next piece of the puzzle—clarifying what, or rather, *who* Joe had meant when he'd warned her not to come back here. For an instant she'd believed she had her answer; instead she had a deeper mystery.

Joe Becket...Jay Barnes...J.B. What was going on?

"You going to stand there and let me bleed to death, or are you going to get out of my way?"

This time she almost welcomed Joe's—*Jay's* rudeness. It helped remind her that until she knew more, she couldn't afford to let him see her confusion.

Hoping he didn't sense her nervousness, too, she reached out again, waiting for him to give her his hand. "As I said, Mr. Barnes, I'm a doctor. By the looks of what you deem as 'care,' it would be in your best interest to let me help."

He seemed on the verge of refusing—and not politely. Beneath his pronounced five o'clock shadow, the naturally taut muscles along his long jaw worked as he ground his teeth together; his midnight-blue eyes narrowed with suspicion, not to mention disapproval.

Maybe he was one of those relics who believed women couldn't be as good as men in any profession, let alone the sciences. She was used to their small-mindedness, and to the type who found her youth disconcerting.

But was that what she felt emanating from Jay Barnes? She didn't think so. She had a hunch he would have been reluctant and rude no matter who was offering him help. It allowed her not to take his rejection personally. It also raised her initial question all over again: Why was he behaving this way?

As pain seemed to win out, he slowly extended his left hand toward her, while the look he shot her warned she better be all she'd advertised.

Rachel ignored that. "Come in here so I can work with better light," she said, stepping back to make room for him.

Once again she sensed his unwillingness, an almost palpable sensation, but at least this time he didn't take forever to make his decision. When he did step forward, she found herself with yet a new problem—she had to deal with the room itself.

Converted years ago from a closet, the bathroom was narrow and cramped, clearly a room designed for no more than one person at a time. Despite the decorating wisdom of crisp white walls and fixtures that helped add a slight sense of space, she had to work to close herself to a surge of claustrophobia.

Hoping he didn't sense her uneasiness, she began unfolding the rag. "Are you in a great deal of pain?"

"Only when someone reminds me of it."

She didn't bother glancing up at him. Didn't dare. "There are reasons for the question besides a concern for your comfort, Mr. Barnes."

"I'd be fine if I hadn't accidentally bumped it."

As the final covering fell away and she saw the angry tear of flesh across the outer edge of his palm, Rachel winced inwardly before replying, "No, you wouldn't. In another twelve to twenty-four hours infection would have set in. What's more, a simple bandage won't get it. You need stitches."

"No stitches."

Neanderthal, she thought, and shot back, "All right, have it your way. I'll do what I can with a pressure bandage and an injection of—"

"You're not giving me any shot, and I'm not paying for one."

Exasperation won ground. "Who asked you to?"

"Don't tell me you'd give me a freebie out of the goodness of your heart?"

"It wouldn't be the first time."

"Uh-huh…that's one way to stay broke."

There was no admiration or approval in his voice, but there wasn't any real scorn, either. Relieved, Rachel replied dryly, "It's been pointed out to me before."

She dropped the offensive rag into the plastic-lined wastebasket and examined the wound. On a small woman or child the cut would have been critical, but on a man of Jay Barnes's tall if lanky size it was slightly less severe. Barely medium height herself, she could tuck herself comfortably under his sharp chin. Not that she had any desire to be there, she amended hastily. She'd just thought that if Joe had stood completely straight, he would be close to that height, too.

Disturbed by her wayward thoughts, she retrieved her bag. "How'd this happen?"

"Working."

"From what I've seen of it, Mr. Beauchamp's establishment is a disaster waiting to happen." Rachel felt him stiffen and glanced up. His expression, if possible, turned more wary than before. Could he suspect her of spying on him? "It's a small town," she said, shrugging. "And you must have figured out by now that our landlady is something of a clearinghouse for all the gossip."

"Don't remind me." Permanent frown lines bisected his straight, stark eyebrows. "So, she mentioned where I worked when she gave you the offical tour of this firetrap?"

His smooth delivery didn't fool her. She could feel tension radiating from him in powerful waves. It made her own overworked nerves feel like gelatin in an earthquake. "She spoke about everyone."

Rachel took a sample tube of antibacterial soap out of her bag. "It's going to sting like crazy, but I need to get the grit washed out of there." To fill the pulsating silence that followed, she said, "I understand you moved in only a short time before I did?"

He grunted from behind compressed lips.

"Well, that's what Adorabella, Mrs. Levieux, told me. But I, um, I don't quite remember where she said you were from?"

"Here and there."

The response, through gritted teeth, could have been a reaction to her work, but Rachel had a hunch it was also a result of another kind of probing. "Really? I enjoy moving around myself. Ever been to Virginia?"

He shook his head.

"That's where I'm from."

"Good for you."

Resemblance or no resemblance, no way he and Joe Becket could be the same man, Rachel thought, repressing a grimace at his continuing rudeness. Jay Barnes acted as though having to be near her was more painful than his hand! And the way he glared…it was a wonder her face wasn't singed from all his searing looks. What did he think she was going to do? she brooded, tugging a few tissues from the dispenser. Stab him with the tube of soap or something?

Who was he and what was going on?

Listen to yourself. One minute she was thinking about the viability of ghosts and the next she was weaving her own dark mystery, all because a withdrawn and more than slightly abrupt neighbor bore a striking resemblance to someone whose blood was, then wasn't, on her hands? *Get a grip, Gentry. Your sense of reality is slipping. Fast.*

"I think that's as dry as it's going to get."

The terse observation made Rachel stop, look and almost groan. Lost in her thoughts, she'd lingered too long over dabbing away the water from the wound. Embarrassed, she tossed the tissues into the trash and dug in her bag for the ointment and the rest of the things she needed.

All she needed was for the man to think she was coming on to him. With a build like his, he probably got more propositions than he knew what to do with, especially if he spent a lot of time walking around in nothing more than unsnapped jeans. "Sorry," she muttered, "it's been a long day."

He didn't bother replying.

Creep. Maybe he had the physique to turn heads,

but he needed a personality transplant to be regarded as human.

For an instant, a shameful instant, she almost wished he and Joe Becket could change places. Why was it always the good ones who got hurt the worst? But as quickly as the thought came, she was overwhelmed with self-disgust.

"This won't sting. In fact, it's quite soothing." As she spoke, she turned back to him and accidentally bumped into his rock-hard bicep. The tube went flying out of her grasp.

Jay Barnes's face was a granite mask as he bent to retrieve it. "Are you sure you're a doctor?"

"Would I be toting this thing around if I wasn't?" she replied, gesturing to her bag.

"Who the hell knows. In any case, you're the clumsiest, edgiest one I've ever met."

"I'm surprised you've known any," she shot back. "In fact, I've about come to the conclusion that you're the type to cauterize your wounds over a flame to prove you're tough and don't need anyone."

"At least I don't put my patients through small-talk hell."

"Listen to who's criticizing—Mr. Personality."

After a slight pause, he replied, "I guess I don't have any room to complain."

His quiet response not only surprised her, it made her uneasy. Maybe it was wishful thinking, but for a moment he almost sounded like... No, she told herself, smoothing ointment on the cut. She wouldn't start that again. "Look, I, um, I've been under considerable stress lately."

"Did it have anything to do with the strange way you behaved when you walked home tonight?"

Her hands shook slightly as she opened a gauze pad and secured it in place with more gauze. "I thought I saw you watching me," she said, when she could control her voice. "Didn't anyone ever tell you it's impolite to spy on other people?"

"I couldn't sleep."

"I'm not surprised."

"Meaning?"

Indignation made her braver, just as it made her fingers more efficient. "It's probably residual guilt over all the people you've fried with your acidic tongue."

"Wrong. Unlike you, most people take the hint when I make it clear I want to be left alone."

"Take heart, Mr. Barnes," she replied, having had enough of this foolishness. "As soon as I finish this, you can go back to your precious privacy with my wholehearted approval."

She worked quickly and without mishap after that, despite being acutely aware of his gaze following her every move. Only when she secured the gauze with a last piece of tape did he break the lengthy silence.

"So, what upset you out there?"

Although outwardly casual, something about the repeated question from a man who had no use for small talk had Rachel's antenna going up again. She decided this time it wouldn't be wise to meet his intense eyes. As it was, they seemed to have X-ray abilities. "Nothing much. I spook easily, that's all."

"People who do don't usually walk home from work at 2:00 a.m."

"They do if they don't own a car," she countered, hoping he'd been awake those times when Cleo had given her a ride. The less she had to explain, the sooner she could change the subject.

But he didn't mention Cleo, or other sightings, seeming interested only in tonight. "It sounded as though the last truck that passed you on the bridge came close to hitting you. Or was there something else?"

She was grateful they were no longer in physical contact, and focused on replacing her things in her bag. "What do you mean?"

"Last week somebody lost a wooden pallet off a flatbed trailer and it messed up a truck's tires before the driver saw it. There've been more than a few animals getting run over up there, too. The fog's treacherous."

"Yes...and actually, it was me the trucker was warning. I, um, was crossing the road and thought I had more time to get out of his way." It wasn't totally a lie. In a way. Even so, Rachel wasn't comfortable with having to shade the truth. She'd worked too hard to keep her life honest and simplified.

"Better be careful," he continued, his tone almost whimsical. "You could get knocked off that thing, fall into the creek, and no one would ever think to look for you down there until it was too late."

"I'll remember that." She didn't know how she got the words out. There was no ignoring that his words could be construed as a slickly phrased threat. Did he have intimate knowledge of such goings-on? Her hand had a fine tremor as she took one last package from her bag. "Well...I'd say we're through. The bandage should be changed within the next twenty-four hours, and I'll give you these." She tried to shove the sample envelope of painkillers into his hand without touching him. "These should take care of any further discomfort you might have."

"I don't take drugs."

"This is very mild. The equivalent of an over-the-counter dosage."

"I don't want them."

She'd had enough. Throwing the pills back in her bag, she zipped it closed. "Fine. If you'll excuse me, I'm dead on my feet and ready for bed."

But he didn't get out of her way. Instead, he tapped the fingers of his good hand against the doorjamb and eyed her with a mixture of doubt and indecision. "Look, I don't mean to be ungrateful, okay? I guess I'm just not the kind of guy who deals with people well."

Whereas Joe Becket had seemed caring and interested. No, no...she didn't want to think about that, about *him* anymore tonight and shook her head dismissively. "We all have our weaknesses."

"I appreciate the first aid."

"You're welcome. Goodnight."

Go, she willed him. But he didn't budge. Unable to avoid it any longer, she looked up and immediately wished she hadn't.

Something changed in his eyes—a flickering of doors inching open, guards being lowered, and wistfulness, maybe even yearning, seeping in. It was as though she was glimpsing the face of another person. It troubled her. In a way, it frightened her...every bit as much as his hard demeanor had. But it also did terrible things to her curiosity.

Unable to resist, she blurted out, "Mr. Barnes...do you by chance have a twin?"

CHAPTER FOUR

"What?"

Rachel told herself that maybe it was time to slow down on the amateur sleuthing. What had she been thinking to challenge him this way when she was physically and psychologically in a vulnerable position?

As for Jay Barnes, all expression vanished from his face. "I don't believe I know what you mean."

"A twin," she said, her boldness waning. "Do you have one?"

"Why do you ask?"

"I'm not sure." She'd noticed that as she grew more uneasy, a deadly calmness had entered his voice. "I suppose it's because I keep getting this feeling we've met before. Do you? Have a twin, I mean?"

"No."

He spun around and walked away. She couldn't say she was disappointed; she simply didn't breathe until she heard the sound of his door shutting. Only then did she expel the breath she'd been holding, shut her eyes and let her clamoring nerves charge through her body like a pinball machine gone haywire.

As soon as she could be sure her legs wouldn't buckle beneath her, she hugged her bag to her chest like a shield and hurried to her room, where she shut the door and bolted it. Only then did she allow herself a shaky sigh of relief.

Things were getting far too complicated. What had she been thinking of to ask him that? She'd as good as told him she was onto him—pure foolishness since she didn't have a clue as to what she was stirring up.

"Well, you're up to your neck in it now," she murmured to herself. The gauntlet had been thrown, leaving her little choice but to figure out what could follow.

Wishing for once that she hadn't been born with a natural curious streak, Rachel placed her bag onto the cane chair beside the door and considered the state of her dubious sanctuary.

When she'd first taken the room, she hadn't minded that its spareness paralleled that of a convent cell, unlike the more ornate ones below. She'd explained to Adorabella that she would be working so much she only needed a place to collapse and sleep off the inevitable fatigue that would be status quo until she fulfilled her contract. Maybe she'd been too hasty.

What was it she'd once heard or read about the simplest room containing any number of weapons? Right—the floral wallpaper could bore Jay Barnes, or whoever he was, to death if she could get him to stand around and stare at it long enough. The lamp on the single, scarred bedside table might be good for one throw. The equally abused dresser held her few toiletries, but most were contained in paper or plastic. She couldn't even count on using the twin-size bed as a hiding place. Strange how until this moment she hadn't noticed its smallness, when even as a child in her family's summer home she'd had a full-size mattress. It showed how tired she really had to be.

Strange, too, that she'd originally taken this room because she'd liked the idea of having a man across the hall—even an unsociable one. Big houses were creaky, and this one wasn't any exception; the sounds of aging often resembled footsteps on the stairs and outside her door.

Adorabella claimed they were the spirits of previous owners. Rachel had smiled politely at that, but had decided she would stick with more logical rationale, like settling boards or the weather. At any rate, she'd claimed Jay Barnes as her invisible, but de facto guardian, and let the knowledge of his presence insulate her confidence in her security.

But now that confidence was shattered. Who was going to protect her from *him* if she had made an exceedingly poor judgment call?

She glanced at the cane chair and, before she could talk herself out of it, moved it under the doorknob. The jiggling and scraping sounds made her wince, but once done she felt slightly better. Confident enough to slip out of her jacket and conscientiously hang it in the starkly bare closet. Then she crossed back to the bed, sprawled onto it and slipped off her shoes.

The cross-stitched bedspread was one Adorabella Levieux had made herself, and it carried the wonderful smell of a fresh laundering. The clean scent also reminded her of the condition of her work clothes. Worried that she might have a drop of blood or street dirt on them, and not wanting to stain the painstakingly made cover, she pushed herself back off the bed. After turning off the light, Rachel stripped off her jeans, blouse and T-shirt in the privacy of near darkness. Then, relying on the faint glow from the security lamps outside, she laid her clothes over the chair and slipped into an oversize shirt.

What now? she thought, facing the shadow-filled

room. No way could she go to sleep after the last
hour's upheaval. Her nerves were stretched tighter
than piano wire and her mind was racing. In fact, she
doubted there would be peace for her before dawn
came, and maybe not even then.

Because it took her farthest from the door, she pad-
ded across the deliciously cool hardwood floor to the
window and curled up on the low, wide ledge.
Through the screen and beyond the gnarled fingers of
the sentinel oaks, night lingered deathly still, as it had
since the mist descended Sunday on Nooton.

From this perspective the bridge took on a surreal
quality. It almost resembled some phantom beast out
of mythical lore—colossal, yet skillfully cloaked by
a vaporous veil of gray. Only a leg showing here, an
ear there, a hint of spine and ominous jaw.

Rachel shivered. Strange visions to conjure—considering she'd never been a fanciful person. And, as
one who had until recently felt well-acquainted, comfortable, with the night, the changes were as depressing as they were unwelcome.

What a mess she'd gotten herself into this time.
She could imagine what her parents would say: *"It's
no less than we expected, Rachel. Only you would
give up all we've provided for you to live in some
backwoods swamp town where the roaches are as big
as domestic animals. Far be it for us to interfere with
your right to live below the poverty line, but did it
ever occur to you to once consider how embarrassing
these selfish gestures are for your family?"*

And yet, if she would ask, they wouldn't hesitate
to do everything in their power to get her on a plane
back to the east coast. Even if it meant calling in
favors from among their Washington, D.C., contacts,

including borrowing a private corporate jet. Nothing would be too good for Phyllis and Earl Gentry's only daughter and youngest child, because Gentrys, they liked to point out, stuck together.

Especially if there was good press involved, Rachel reflected bitterly.

But she also knew any favor extended to her would come with a price tag. One she wouldn't pay, regardless of her anxiety over what she might have gotten herself into. She'd worked too hard for her independence to hand it back to them, even if it looked slightly stress-fractured at the moment. Eleven years' hard, she thought, remembering Roddie. An old, familiar pain gripped her heart. There was another reason to stand firm: if she surrendered and ran home, it would be turning her back on what her brother had died for.

Gestures, indeed. No, she would have to see this situation through on her own. But never had she felt more unsure of herself or about what to do.

Trying to think back to the beginning, she rested her forehead on her updrawn knees. *Think about Joe.... Joe warning you about...who? Jay Barnes, who looked like him, but couldn't be him?* It didn't make any sense! Jay Barnes was no more Joe Becket than she was Princess Whatshername. His unignorable physique versus her sexually deprived status aside, there had been no real chemistry between them.

Except for that one moment when...

None, she argued with herself, repressing her mutinous thoughts. While on the other hand, Joe, with a few simple words, a look and a caress had made her feel...special...needed...wanted.

Bright Eyes. Like a whisper carried on the night's

steady wing, the memory of his voice, as well as his words, floated to her. No one had ever called her that before. Being a woman who'd gone through college, graduate school, medical training and hell's internship in her own noncomformist way, she was too experienced to fall for negligent flattery. Two affairs had also left her dubious as to whether she was capable of opening her heart again. But how often did a woman have a ghost tell her he needed to touch her more than he wanted his dubious contact with the world?

"Only you don't *believe* in the supernatural," she whispered.

Torn, Rachel leaped to her feet and combed both hands through her hair.

So what was going on? Maybe she needed to focus on things from a different angle...specifically, on someone who didn't vanish the moment she touched him...which brought her back to Jay Barnes.

She pressed her lips together. Not for a moment did she believe that man. She also didn't think his reticence had anything to do with a penchant for privacy. He was hiding from something, or someone, she knew it.

How strange his expression had been when she'd asked about a twin. She'd only posed the question because she couldn't think of any other way to explain his uncanny similarity to Joe. Obviously, she'd touched a tender nerve. All she had to do was figure out what it was.

From the moment he'd first seen her, he'd known she would be trouble for him. It gave him no pleasure to have her prove him right.

As he lay on his bed with sleep farther away than ever, he linked his hands behind his head and swore at the stabbing pain. That damned hand would be his downfall yet!

Shifting to avoid putting any further weight on it, he again berated himself for being a clumsy fool. He'd injured himself trying to keep Mudcat's building from falling around him, holding up sheet metal paneling as he'd reached for the drill. There was, however, no such thing as a successful shortcut—at least, not for him. He'd discovered that as a kid when he'd written a book report based on the cover jacket and received a failing mark; he'd had the lesson drilled into him every time impatience or pride had lured him into beating around the bush instead of doing something the right way. Now his throbbing hand reiterated the old lesson.

At least the derisive and damnably desirable doctor had been right about the ointment. The burning had about stopped. But the thing was still stinging like a nest of vengeful scorpions.

Dr. Rachel Gentry...what was he going to do about her? He'd never doubted the legitimacy of her credentials; however, just as there were cops who were crooked and politicians who were worse, he figured it was entirely feasible for a doctor—especially one who was so easy on the eyes—to be not quite on the up-and-up. What else explained what a woman with her understated class was doing in a moldy sinkhole like Nooton?

He'd known her name almost from the moment she'd moved in. The Duchess had told him when he'd gone downstairs to pay for another month's rent. He'd let the drifty old landlady lure him into her parlor—

crammed with everything except spiderwebs—and prattle to her heart's content. It had been a sacrifice considering the god-awful cologne she doused herself with. The mere thought of how the artificial sweetness had conflicted with the strange smells drifting out from the kitchen made him shudder. But he'd sat and listened, her voice reminding him of a scratched-up vinyl record.

"...Dr. Rachel Gentry of the Washington Gentrys. I'm sure you've heard of them." He hadn't. "Oh, my dear, impeccable lineage. They're connected to the Georgia Gentrys, you know. Rachel—she insists I call her Rachel, isn't that sweet?—well, Rachel inherited that delightful complexion that's become world renown. But I digress..."

She'd about digressed him into a coma. These days he couldn't afford to give a damn about the hide on peaches, women or anything else; he had been pleased that he'd come away with enough information to justify his uneasiness about his new neighbor.

Rachel Gentry, he'd concluded, might be a legitimate physician, but she was no more a good Samaritan doing her bit for the underprivileged in this parish than he was the pope's son. He would have to stay alert until she made her move.

Pity she was such a looker, though, and sharp. That had probably been the idea—send in the primo bait to sniff him out. He'd never made it a secret that he had an appreciation for independent women who had as much brainpower as beauty. Someone must have tipped them off and they'd decided to test the theory, since nothing else seemed to be working in their attempt to locate and flush him out.

Well, let them try. He enjoyed a game of cat and

mouse as much as anyone, and he'd been getting more than a little restless, anyway. How the devil did Garth stand it around here? he wondered, then reminded himself that the snake lived on an estate surrounded with all the toys other people's money could buy.

Feeling a new surge of bitterness, he jackknifed off the bed and paced the confines of his room. Room—ha! he thought with a new surge of sarcasm. The price of obtaining privacy had meant taking this man-size version of a toaster oven. Fog or no fog, the temperature remained lethal up here regardless of the hour, and the closest thing to air-conditioning crazy Adorabella provided was the oscillating fan on the dresser. Most of the time he refused to run it, because the ancient thing had almost no safety guard left and sounded as though it was still busy grinding up fingers of previous tenants.

He stopped before it, tempted to turn it on despite all the reasons he shouldn't. He was drenched with sweat, and the hot, humid breeze would have to feel better than this. Of course, best of all would be a beer.

If he had to stay here much longer, he was going to have to look into getting one of those small refrigerators and a quiet fan...and then he could wile away the hours by wondering if he would live long enough to get his money's worth out of them.

He reached for his cigarettes and lighter, reminding himself for the umpteenth time that life was easier without complications. Maybe somebody should have told bright-eyed Dr. Gentry that. Hell, she seemed too young to have her license, let alone be involved in this kind of filth.

His cigarettes and lighter lay beside the man-eating

fan. Pulling one from the pack, he stopped it inches away from his mouth, then slammed it back onto the dresser. Down to almost three a day and she'd nearly ruined it for him.

He ran his good hand over his hair. Like the rest of him, it was soaking wet, another warning that he was edging toward an explosion.

What the hell, he thought, thinking about the beer again. Hadn't he already reserved himself a first-class ticket to hell? He might as well make it a worthwhile trip.

He headed for the door.

CHAPTER FIVE

He thought his door might well be the only one in the house that didn't squeak when opened. Humidity served as the culprit. With all the windows lifted to invite reluctant breezes, it had its run of the place. But he'd offset its effect on the hinges by keeping them oiled. As a result, when he eased out of his room and paused in the hall, he did so in near silence.

As was the case in his own room, the only light came from the blue-gray glow seeping through the window at the end of the hall. Because he lived in the darkness as much as he could in order to develop his night vision, he didn't mind.

He took a moment to listen at Rachel Gentry's door. There was a brief rustling and a squeak—as she turned in her bed?—followed by stillness. Without consciously intending to, he found himself picturing her as she slept, or rather the way he preferred to imagine her...wearing only the night's wet kiss, her slim body graceful in a half twist like a ballerina in midleap, her hands lost in the dark silk of her hair. Just as unintentionally came the stirrings of arousal heating his body.

Like he needed this, he thought, berating himself for his weakness. He couldn't afford to keep letting his thoughts drift to her, regardless of whether it made the hours of isolation pass more quickly or not. She already had too much of an effect on him, and that could prove problematic if things started coming apart.

Thirstier than ever, he made his way down the hall, treating the carpet runner like a serpent to be avoided. He'd learned that if he stayed on either the left or right side of it, he could usually reach the stairs without making a sound. It had become another game to him—a potentially lifesaving one. He'd taught himself the tone of each creak, too. Now when he heard someone coming, he knew exactly where they were positioned and who they were by their weight displacement on the hardwood floor.

But because of the relentless effects of the dampness combined with the age of the house, it was impossible even for him to get through without at least one squeak, and he found it, a new one, three feet in front of the landing. Silently cursing, he made a mental note of the spot.

The stairs were supposed to be easier because he'd learned to balance the bulk of his weight by resting his right hand on the railing, his left against the wall, and using a variation of a sailor's method of descent in a ship. Under the circumstances, however, that maneuver was impossible, and the childlike tactic of sliding down on the railing wasn't going to work, either, if he couldn't easily stop himself. Deciding he needed the discipline, he started down the hard way.

Once he reached the second floor, he knew he could move more swiftly without having to worry about noise. The codger on this level snored loud enough to block out any noise he made, and no doubt the divorcee had yet to return from her nightly manhunt. But at the first level, he stopped.

There was something about this part of the house

that bothered him. Something odd. If he put any merit in his landlady's prattling, he would blame it on the spooks she claimed roamed around here. On the other hand, he'd met the voodoo queen, her housekeeper, and he figured she was the one who left him feeling he had a bull's-eye painted at the base of his neck.

Even so, he enjoyed his periodic raids down here to swipe something from Jewel's refrigerator. He never touched the food, though, no matter how hungry he was. Most of it looked strange enough to persuade him to turn down the Duchess's frequent invitations to "family" dinners. The voodoo queen did, however, share his appreciation for beer, even if hers was a cheap local brand.

That's what he'd come down for, and upon reaching the refrigerator, conspicuous by its modernness in a kitchen that was otherwise a throwback to forty, maybe fifty years ago, he carefully opened the right-hand door. The room filled with light and, uncomfortable, he quickly reached for a can on the bottom shelf. That's when he felt it.

It had happened before, although never this powerfully. The only way to describe the intense awareness was that it felt like being in the cross hairs of the scope of a powerful rifle zeroing in on his skull. Without so much as drawing a breath, he dove beside the refrigerator, letting the door continue swinging open. It swept the huge kitchen with a yellow light, and he saw...

Nothing. Nothing at all. Except that the curtains, hung in lieu of a pantry door, were shifting. From the breeze of the swinging refrigerator door, he told himself.

Maybe.

He shifted to a crouch, then rose to his feet. He took a step forward, a knot of tension hardening in his gut, and then took another. With every expectation of a barrel appearing and discharging into his midsection, he grabbed both sides of the curtain and yanked it open.

"Jeez." He backed away in shock and disgust.

Rachel jerked upright in bed, an unpleasant feeling, at once frightening and disorienting. But knowing the sensations passed more quickly when she didn't fight them, she leaned back against the headboard and waited, completely still and silent, until the jumpiness and nausea passed. And to gain some insight into why she'd been jarred to consciousness this time.

Her mouth felt as though someone had stuffed it with the down from her pillows. Her shirt clung to her perspiration-dampened body like an unwelcome hand. Convinced that nothing more than the oppressive weather had intruded on her sleep again, she leaned over and checked the time.

Dismayed to see she hadn't been asleep for even an hour yet, she kicked off the sheet tangled around her legs. At this rate she would be a basket case within the next week, she moaned silently, brushing hair out of her face and climbing out of bed. She went to the window to see if anything had changed—if there was a chance of a shower or a breeze. Something had to give, even if neither of those possibilities looked likely.

What unholy weather. That wasn't only her opinion—everyone was saying so. Normally, a number of natives had explained to her, something would give one way or another. The logical ones blamed the persistent fog on global warming. A few strange characters pointed to UFO interference, the coming of the Age of Aquarius or Armageddon. Rachel saw logic in the theory about the troubled environment, but her instincts were edging toward a conclusion even stranger than the UFO idea.

"No more," she moaned, massaging her temples with her fingertips. "Not tonight."

Maybe a cup of water and two aspirin would relax her enough to get back to sleep. Shifting to massage her neck, she headed for the door. If she didn't get some rest, Sammy was going to give her heck when she went in to relieve him in the afternoon. That kind of trouble she didn't need. Up to this point in her career, she'd managed to show all her supervisors that she could handle her share of job stress; she wasn't about to prove otherwise.

After moving the chair, she was about to free the secondary lock on her door, when she froze. What was that? A footstep?

She pressed her ear closer to the door and listened. For a moment everything remained silent, and then…it wasn't exactly a step she heard, but a slight shifting of the floorboards, as though someone was trying to hide their movements.

Could it be Jay Barnes? What was he doing up?

The question was, how could anyone sleep in this sauna?

Rachel shut her eyes and tried to think. Maybe his hand hurt him worse than he'd admitted.

No doubt he's been lying about a number of things, but if you open that door you may find out more than is healthy to know.

It was a risk she felt she needed to take. She'd had

enough of trying to answer her own questions. Too many of them were being left unexplained. But that didn't mean she wouldn't be careful.

Ever so cautiously, she slid back the lock. Seeing how her hands were shaking, she quickly released the other lock and swung the door open.

A dark figure sprang toward her, had probably begun to do so the instant he'd heard the door opening. He moved with a speed and agility that Rachel found terrifying. She gasped and fell back against her opened door. With nowhere to go, she waited for the inevitable.

But rather than attack, he rested a hand on the right side of her head and growled, "What do you think you're doing?"

Fair question—if she'd been in the mood to be fair. "*Me?* What are *you* doing? Have you any idea what a fright—You could've hurt me!"

"If I'd meant to, you wouldn't be standing."

His cold confidence made her stare in mute disbelief. She forgot how hot she was and how brave she'd always believed she could be in the face of adversity. All she knew was that she'd made a ridiculously big mistake by opening the door. "You're a very strange man, Mr. Barnes," she replied, deciding to salvage what was left of her common sense and retreat. Fast. "If you'll excuse me…"

With a mere shifting of his weight, he blocked her with his left shoulder. "Not so fast."

The maneuver brought him so close she could feel the heat of his half-naked body merging with her own. It created a near-electric aura between them. Barely able to move her lips, Rachel whispered, "Please get out of my way."

"After you answer some questions."

"If anyone should be answering questions, it's you. I'm not the one creeping around out there."

"Aren't you?"

"Of course not."

"You're saying you've been in here all along?"

"Yes. Why?"

"Never mind."

"Did you hear something before? Please tell me. I'd thought I'd heard something, too."

"Do you always open your door at night to check on strange sounds?" he asked, his cool sarcasm running over her words.

She drew a deep, controlling breath. "No, of course not. I suppose I assumed it was you. I thought maybe you were feeling worse and might need help."

"Help." His gaze slid downward and he curled his lips, but there was nothing amused or congenial about the smile. "Exactly what did you have in mind?"

A scorching fever swept through her, growing less ignorable with each second he continued to stare. Unable to resist, she glanced downward herself and groaned inwardly.

No wonder he was treating her as though she'd propositioned him. During her brief, restless sleep, two buttons on her shirt had opened, leaving a gaping slash that couldn't look more suggestive if she'd tried.

Well, there was no sense in pretending it hadn't happened. Forcing herself to match him stare for stare, she buttoned up, drawling, "If you've seen enough?"

"Do you really want an answer?"

"No," she replied coolly, fighting to ignore the sensations churning within her. It was because he looked so much like Joe Becket, she told herself. What she felt for Jay Barnes, however, was sheer, unadulterated dislike. "About your hand, does it hurt?"

"I feel it."

"And that's your remedy?" she asked, nodding to the can he lifted to his mouth.

"It beats the stuff coming out of our water taps. You look a little warm yourself—want a swallow?"

She eyed the can, thought about placing her lips where his had been, and her temperature rose another few degrees. "No, thank you."

"What's the matter? Afraid? I don't have anything you have to worry about catching."

She was afraid, period…of him, of herself, of what was happening every second their gazes held. "I simply don't care for any, that's all."

Jay Barnes gave a brief shake of his head. "Where did they find you?"

Lost, she frowned. "Pardon?"

"Forget it. Let's just say, I'm game if you are, *Doctor.*"

She didn't understand a thing he was saying, but she understood an intimated insult when she heard one. "Mr. Barnes, I'm beginning to believe that if there's a game being played, so far only you know the rules."

"And that's how I intend to keep it. All you need to understand is that if you want to save that gorgeous neck of yours, you'd better beat it while you still have a chance."

She couldn't believe what she was hearing. "I work here!"

His gaze swept over her one more time and lingered on her mouth. "Fine," he growled, finally pushing away from the door. "Have it your own way."

CHAPTER SIX

He filled her dreams, so vivid a presence that when Rachel awoke from hearing the door closing, she again bolted upright in bed, expecting to see him standing before her. Once she realized it was daylight and the sound was Jay Barnes leaving for work, she fell back against her sweat-dampened pillows and stared up at the fine cobweb design of the ceiling's cracking plaster.

Exhaustion left her feeling drained, numb. Maybe with him out of the house she could finally get a few hours of decent rest. But some rebellious part of her mind began to rapidly churn out thoughts and images; she remembered disturbing snatches of dreams, such as the way she'd called him ''Joe''...how she'd let him undo the last button on her nightshirt...let him slip his hands inside...touch her...make love to her.

Her conscious, conservative side didn't like that at all. He wasn't Joe, she reminded herself with brutal censure. He couldn't be. And as for Joe... Oh, God, what about him? What was he? *Why* was he?

With that mystery plaguing her again, she abandoned any hope of going back to sleep and dragged her sluggish body to the bathroom for a tepid shower. She reasoned it would at least cool her feverish body, if not her steamy thoughts.

Minutes later, refreshed, but nursing a headache, she returned to her room. Blow-drying her shoulder-length pageboy took another block of time, thanks to the humidity's stubborn effect on her hair. Stretching exercises to ease knots of tension took a bit more.

Finally, she pulled on her usual uniform of jeans and a shirt—white cotton as usual, in hopes of making herself feel cooler—and made her way downstairs. But for all her efforts, she still felt as though she'd never been to bed.

Not much time had passed, either. The ornate grandfather clock in the foyer confirmed what her wristwatch indicated: it was barely past nine. Late enough for Adorabella to have roused herself, though, which was why she'd come down. Hopefully Jewel was serving coffee. But upon reaching the formal dining room, Rachel found it vacant. The elegant table, resplendent with an antique-lace tablecloth, bore the crystal bowl Adorabella liked to use as a vase. Today it was filled with red roses. The victims, plucked from the lush bushes out back, looked only slightly better than she felt.

She groaned inwardly, aware of what it all meant. If she wanted coffee, she would have to try the kitchen.

No one wandered into Jewel's domain without an invitation; Adorabella had warned her of that during the grand tour. Rachel had taken the old woman at her word and had avoided the place ever since, although more out of respect for Jewel's privacy than from any real concern for her own well-being. Everyone deserved privacy, she'd told herself, especially housekeepers with a penchant for black magic. Even rude neighbors, she added, her thoughts inevitably straying toward Jay Barnes.

With a sharp shake of her head, she decided she would be better off going to the café. It was too hot to think about food, but she had to get something into her system. Most appealing was that at the café the most stressful thing she would have to deal with was whether to have cereal or a bran muffin.

But before she could retreat, the door between the kitchen and dining room swung open, and a white-and-green-turbaned head appeared around the edge. Brown eyes, so dark they appeared black, drove into her like twin stakes. "You going to stand there the rest of the morning or you gonna come in?" Jewel demanded in a melodious alto.

Staring at the rounded, broad-planed face that looked more like forty than the sixty-something Adorabella claimed was Jewel's true age, Rachel thought it might be fascinating to learn if Jewel really could see out the back of her head, as well as through walls. On the other hand, Rachel's world was already overwhelmed with mystery and mayhem—did she need to be taking on any new challenges?

"Actually," she began, taking a step backward, "I was about to—"

"I done poured your coffee. C'mon."

As fast as it had appeared, the head withdrew, leaving the door to swing back and forth like a beckoning hand. Rachel wiped her palms on her jeans and advanced toward unknown territory.

From the moment Adorabella had introduced her to her tall, bone-thin housekeeper, Rachel had felt an undeniable awe. Because of the control in the older woman's eyes, she'd told herself. She'd never known anyone with more confidence than Jewel Bonnard, reverentially called "Widow Jack" by almost everyone else in town. That nickname was a result of being the longtime widow of the unfortunate "Handsome

Jack'' Bonnard, as well as the parish's most cele-
brated hoodoo woman.

Rachel had heard the first of many outlandish tales
about Adorabella Levieux's longtime companion and
employee at the café. Because of Jack's roving eye
and philandering ways, Jewel had been influential in
his early demise. The law never filed charges—fear
of being hexed themselves, some insisted. That story
proved to be the cornerstone of her theory that Nooton was hardly the innocuous hamlet it appeared to
be.

Having no idea what she was walking into, she
pushed open the kitchen door. On the other hand, she
reasoned, could anyone truly prepare for a close encounter with a *voodooeinne?*

The kitchen was larger than some dance floors
she'd seen, no doubt built to accommodate the lavish
entertaining that was reputed to have gone on in the
house decades ago. Jewel made it her own place by
scent alone. Rachel tried not to react to the malodor-
ous concoction simmering on the great stove on the
opposite side of the room, certain she didn't want to
know whether it was a cure or a curse.

"Are you sure I'm not taking you away from anything?"

"Just washing the evilness out of these sheets."
Jewel stirred the contents of the black cauldron, her
size-twelve feet planted solidly in a pair of men's
leather loafers. "Promised Miss Adorabella I'd make
the she-cat see the error of her ways."

"I...see." Rachel guessed this had something to
do with the divorcée on the second floor. Cecilie—
no Celia something-or-other. Maybe the less she

knew about *that* story the better. "I suppose Mrs. Levieux isn't up yet?"

"Won't be until noon. Sit."

Rachel took a seat at the chrome-edged table where a cup of pitch-colored, steaming coffee indeed waited. "That's late even for her. She didn't overdo it with the pills?"

"Told you about them, did she?"

"The bottle fell from her pocket one day while we were chatting." Rachel added a little sugar to her coffee before tasting it. She didn't usually, but it was a potent-looking brew. Besides, she reasoned, extra energy wouldn't hurt either. "You're aware they're sleeping pills, aren't you, Jewel?"

"Who do you think went with her the first time the prescription needed filling?"

Rachel moistened her lips. "Aren't you concerned about her mixing alcohol with drugs?"

"I've been taking care of her for years and years," Jewel replied, without turning around. "Ain't nothing gonna happen to her until the Lord calls her home."

It took what little patience Rachel had left not to explode. But she'd seen too many deaths that were a result of exactly this to keep silent. "Faith is a wonderful thing. But, Jewel, we're talking about a potentially lethal combination here."

"Nothing lethal about baby aspirin. Not in the doses I give her."

Rachel had been lifting the cup to her lips...and stopped it an inch away. "I beg your pardon?"

"She's been taking baby aspirin for three years now and ain't figured out the difference yet. Also been weakening her drink with peach juice. I know my business," she added, shooting her a sidelong look. "Knew it long before you were sucking on your mama."

It was on the tip of Rachel's tongue to drolly inform the woman that her mother had never let anyone get that close to her, but she decided the technicality was insignificant to the lesson learned. Not knowing whether to be relieved or amused, she covered the awkward silence by finally tasting the coffee. It was as strong as she'd suspected, but welcome.

"It would seem I owe you an apology," Rachel murmured at last.

"You're just young, child. Ain't nothing for me to take offense over."

So much for backhanded compliments, Rachel mused, glancing out the window on her left and sighing at the fog. "Well, at least someone is getting some rest. I don't know how she does it in this weather, though."

"Easy enough. I fixed her an apple. Always fix her one when I got too much work and need her out from underfoot." With her wooden spoon, Jewel spun the red fruit hanging above the steaming pot.

Rachel had noticed the piece of fruit before, but she'd thought it a useless attempt to offset the putrid smell rising from the pot. "I don't understand." Despite the offensive odor, she rose and, with cup and saucer in hand, approached the stove for a closer look.

The apple hung from somewhere inside the hood by a thin nylon line. It looked as though it had been cored and then put together again. "You're saying that's what's making her sleep?"

"Never fails. You write a name on a piece of paper and put it inside the hole. Thing is, you're supposed to hang it over rising smoke. Ain't got no smoke this time of the year, so I got to improvise. Don't matter, though, if you got the power. The steam gets thick, her eyes get heavy and…'' Jewel tapped her wooden spoon against the side of the pot.

The tinny sound had Rachel blinking and backing away. "And that's it?"

"Why complicate things?" There was no missing a certain glint in Jewel's eye as the older woman glanced over a bony shoulder at her. "You ain't sleeping worth three winks lately. Want me to fix you one?"

"Ah…no. But thank you."

"You don't believe."

She considered making some vague statement about scientific studies on the power of suggestion, but decided against it. No matter what she believed, she didn't want to offend Jewel, and so she opted for a more subjective response. "Looking tired is an occupational hazard. I'll catch up on my sleep…"

"Once the fog lifts, eh?"

Her words caused goose bumps to rise on Rachel's arms. "Something like that. I've had a great deal to cope with these past few days. And you're right, the weather doesn't help."

Jewel pursed her lips, which elongated her cheekbones, giving her an even stronger Egyptian look than Rachel had noticed before. "Know what I think? I think he's making you nervous, that one is."

The cup and saucer rattled in her hands. "I'm afraid I don't know…who?"

Once again the housekeeper used the spoon to point, this time at the ceiling.

The oddest conflicting wave of relief and anxiety

swept over Rachel. She'd expected the strange woman to point out the window at the bridge. On the other hand, the direction she chose was equally unsettling. "Mr. Barnes," she murmured, making some quick choices. "Jewel...what do you know about him?"

"He's got the spirits all stirred." She gestured behind Rachel. "Prayed to Black Hawk about him. Asked him to make Jay Barnes go. But that one's power's strong."

Having no idea who Black Hawk was, Rachel turned and—gasped. She'd seen some shocking, even horrific, things in her career so far, but this was... As she fought back her revulsion, the cup and saucer wobbled in her hands. It sent hot liquid spilling over her fingers, burning her. Unable to hold on, she let the china crash to the floor.

Across the room on a shelf in the pantry, framed by parted drapes in the same material as Jewel's turban, was a shrine of some sort. But to whom—no, to *what*—she had no idea. The hideous black figurine was surrounded by candles, feathers and assorted pots, and things she couldn't begin to identify, nor did she want to.

Tearing her gaze away, she focused on the mess she'd made and quickly stooped to begin cleaning it up. "I'm so sorry. I'm not normally clumsy. Let me—ah!"

A sliver of porcelain cut the tip of her finger. As she watched, a streak of blood spread across a piece of white china. It seemed to fascinate Jewel, too. The woman descended with a speed that defied her age and snatched up the piece from the floor.

Staring at it, Jewel moaned softly. "Spilling of innocent blood. I knew it. It's no good. No good."

Her distress made Rachel want to assure her. "It's really all right. Look, there's barely a scratch. I'll just run upstairs and rinse it off."

"Stay away from him."

Halfway to the door, and eager to escape, Rachel was compelled to turn around. "What did you say?"

"He's spilled blood before. He'll do it again. Yours, if you're not careful. Stay away."

"How do you... No, that's preposterous."

But Jewel wasn't listening. "I'll give you strong magic," she said urgently. "Powerful. Maybe it's not too late." She hurried to the shrine and brought out what appeared to be a ball of black wax. "Here. Take this and work it flat. Then write his name on a piece of paper. Write it four times front ways and five times back. *Listen* to me."

The force of her grip had Rachel gasping. "Jewel!"

"You remember what I'm telling you. Put the paper in the middle of the wax and roll it up into a ball again. Then you go to the bridge and you throw it. Downstream, hear? Away from town. Far as you can."

Rachel shook her head and attempted to pull away from the strong hands that were trying to press the slick object into hers. "No. Please."

"Take it."

Successful on her next attempt to free herself, Rachel backed away. "I'm sorry," she whispered, and bolted from the room.

"Fool!" Jewel's shout followed her. "You'll be sorry!"

Will be? Rachel thought, fighting back an incredulous laugh as she raced up the stairs. She already was—for not following her first impulse and going to the café. She didn't need this added lunacy.

By the time she reached the bathroom, the tiny cut had stopped bleeding. In fact, it looked ludicrously insignificant to have raised so much of a fuss. After rinsing the scratch clean, Rachel didn't even bother using a bandage to protect it. She wasn't, however, as fortunate at stemming the flow of her thoughts.

Jewel was crazy, she assured herself. A demented old woman who'd gotten away with too much for too long.

But she seemed to have pegged Jay Barnes correctly, didn't she?

Rachel covered her ears and shut her eyes tight. She needed to talk to somebody. Someone solid, sensible...sane.

At this point she could think of only one person around here who qualified.

CHAPTER SEVEN

"Man, I love this weather."

Sucking in a deep breath that expanded his torso to barrel proportions, Dwight Beauchamp stood beneath the first of two overhead doors at Beauchamp's Gas and Body Works, smacking his wide, thick lips. It was that mouth, along with his somewhat flat head and wide-spaced eyes, that had earned him the dubious nickname "Mudcat" from his teammates in high school football. In the twenty-five years since, he'd explained to Jay Barnes during one of his frequent excursions into nostalgia, almost every one of his teammates had ended up needing his car repaired here. If fate was willing to dole out that kind of retribution, he told him, who was he to complain about a little teasing?

Remembering the story, Jay had an idea he knew just how much Mudcat appreciated the weather, so he kept his ascerbic opinion about the dismal climatic conditions to himself. Instead he continued checking his paint gun and hose connections.

"Yessiree," Mudcat continued, "it feels like another fender-bender day. Nothing better than working steeped in the sweet aroma of money in the making, ain't that right, J.B.? Look at that thick gumbo out there. Ain't it beautiful? Man, it's beautiful."

Jay hated Mudcat using his initials, and he was getting fed up with his nonstop babbling, as well. In an effort to escape both, he dropped the paint hood—

which also protected him from fumes—over his face, and began spraying the base coat on the section of the semi's cab they were repairing. *He* was repairing. Now that Mudcat had himself an official "Body Works Department"—more like a token slave, considering the salary Jay had let himself be hired for— he was playing the role of boss for all it was worth. All he lacked was the stereotypical fat cigar.

Mudcat, Jay fumed to himself. *What kind of man let himself be called anything so asinine?*

But even as he griped, he knew it had nothing to do with what was really eating at him. Sure, the guy was ninety percent hot air, but working here provided Jay with a job within walking distance to the boardinghouse—an important technicality, since he'd hitched his way out here in order to leave his car in Houston. No, it wasn't Mudcat's fault he was so hot under the collar. It was the woman who was pushing his wrong buttons...and if she kept it up, she was going to learn how few he had left.

After working only a short while, and blinded by the sting of sweat running into his eyes, Jay turned away from the cloud of paint to draw fresh air into his lungs. For a few seconds it felt almost cool compared to what he'd been inhaling under the hood.

How the hell did anyone do this for a living year in and year out? he wondered, using the rag in the back pocket of his jeans to wipe the streams of perspiration from his face. Was he doing an adequate job of convincing his boss that he knew the business? Like most men, he'd grown up enjoying messing around with cars. A few of his old man's buddies had even taught him a thing or two about bodywork. But a pro he wasn't, and since taking this job he'd been banking on the hunch that Mudcat wasn't one, either.

He glanced around, looking for the guy, and saw that he'd gone back into his air-conditioned office and parked his bulk behind his desk. His executive chair looked as though it had been salvaged from the local dump, Jay thought, watching him return to his favorite pastime, namely jabbering away on the phone. Now *there* was the one thing Mudcat was good for. The man's love of gabbing kept him preoccupied most of the day. Of course, that also left *Jay* with most of the work.

With a shake of his head, Jay shoved the rag back into his back pocket. He had to get a grip—his nerves were stretching way too thin. Maybe he'd be in better shape if he knew how much longer it would be before he finished here... and what the final outcome would be. A too-familiar scent of death seemed to be a constant presence these days, filling his nostrils with every breath. It was making him edgier. The Gentry woman was making things worse.

He tried, but he couldn't forget the way she'd stared at him. She'd looked as though she'd seen a ghost. It could mean only one thing: she had to be one of Garth's people... which also meant he might have to get rid of her. The idea wasn't pleasant to contemplate, but if it came down to making a choice between him or her, he knew what decision he would have to make.

The bell sounding the arrival of a customer jerked him out of his dark brooding. Glancing over his shoulder, he saw the late-model four-door pull up to the gas pumps. He set down the spray gun, about to tug his hood completely off his head because he knew

Mudcat wasn't likely to get off his butt and take care of the customer himself. Then he recognized the blond-haired guy sitting on the passenger side of the front seat. Instead of removing the hood, he dropped it back in place, snatched up the paint gun and turned back to the truck.

Damn. He knew the guy with the burr haircut and was already thinking about what he could use as a weapon or how he could escape if he, in turn, was identified. No way he could go out the front way without being spotted.

"Hey, J.B.? Customer!"

Mudcat's voice carried through the glass door so clearly, it might as well have been screen mesh. Jay grit his teeth and willed him to keep his big mouth shut.

"J.B.!"

The driver of the sedan sounded his horn, but Jay knew he had no choice; he had to ignore it. He pretended to inspect the portion of the cab he'd already painted, then started spraying again.

When Mudcat burst from the office, Jay could feel his agitation across the garage. It took considerable concentration as the man stomped over and grabbed his shoulder, for Jay to not whip around and shove Mudcat's nose up into his skull.

Instead, he pretended to be dumbfounded, shut off the spray gun and maneuvered so that he had his back turned to the car. "What's up?"

"You gone deaf? Customer's waiting!"

"The compressor's running and I've got this hood on. I didn't know."

"Well, now you do. Go take care of them."

"Can't. You'd better handle it."

Mudcat gave him a pained look. "I'm the boss, J.B. I'm the one who's supposed to say who does what around here."

"You want this done right?" Jay asked, with a shrug of indifference. "I can't do both. Not if you expect a smooth finish."

"But it ain't the way it's supposed to—" Again the horn sounded. "Aw, hell. All right. This time. But you'd better do a damned good job, hear?" Mudcat grumbled, already stomping toward the sedan.

That had been a close one. As relief surged through him, Jay once again dropped the hood in place and turned back to the truck. That's when he saw the stream of primer running down the side. He swore under his breath, hoping he could fix it before Mudcat saw it.

Mudcat did see it less than five minutes later. As the sedan pulled away, the stout man huffed and puffed over to him, complaining all the louder when he reached Jay. "We need to talk, man. This ain't right. See, I was on the phone, and when I'm doing business, you're supposed to— Holy dipstick. What's that? I thought you said you were an expert. My old lady did a better job painting our house, and she was seven months pregnant!"

Fed up with playing subordinate to the guy, Jay decided enough was enough. "I'm sorry, okay? I hit my bad hand and overcompensated."

"I'll say you did." Mudcat poked his finger into Jay's arm. "You'd better be more careful, J.B., 'cause I ain't—"

Like a pit bull suddenly unleashed, Jay sprung into action. He grabbed the man's wrist and bent it in a way that left nothing to the imagination as to what would happen next. "Don't," he warned with deceptive softness. "If you ever want to use this again, don't touch me."

"H-hey, hold on, man."

"If it wasn't for this dump falling down around me and my effort to bolt that siding back in place for you yesterday, I wouldn't be working with one hand and we wouldn't be having this conversation." He leaned into Mudcat's face. "So maybe you'll want to be careful about how hard you push me. Agreed?"

Mudcat turned slightly green around the gills, then a ruddy, rash red. Jay hoped the guy hadn't been scared into having a stroke. Life was complicated enough at the moment.

"Okay, man. Cool down. I hear you." As soon as Jay released him, Mudcat raced for the safety of his office. At the door, he spun around. "But make sure you get it right next time!"

Jay didn't bother waiting for the door to slam. More interested in making sure the sedan had left, he stepped outside and searched for it. He spotted the vehicle just starting across the bridge. Apparently it had been slowed by traffic.

Although the mist was at its thickest over Black Water Creek, he immediately noted the car wasn't the only thing out there. Someone was walking, too. A woman.

The sedan's taillights flared and the car slowed. Stopped. Jay felt a tightening in his belly. Mist or no mist, he'd grown extremely familiar with that particular form and the casual grace with which it moved.

Garth's people had stopped for Miss Class Act herself...Dr. Rachel Gentry. Did he know his business, or what?

* * *

She'd been concentrating so intently, wondering if she might be able to detect something, *anything* at this point, on the bridge, that Rachel didn't notice the car until it had eased up beside her. It gave her a jolt, and her heart did a second plunge when she recognized the man rolling down the passenger window.

Even if she couldn't have remembered his name after their one meeting, she would never forget his sly, toothy grin. Just as the first time she'd been exposed to it, she again found it unnerving.

"Morning, Rachel."

Wade Maddox's quick familiarity had her feeling more uneasy. It reminded her of the night he brought in a so-called friend to the clinic, whom, he'd explained, had gotten into a fight. The friend had looked more like a victim of an intentional beating. Every bone in his right hand had been broken, and the tip of one finger had been severed. When she'd insisted they report the incident to the police, he'd stopped her. He'd been polite, even amused, but the look in his pale blue eyes had made it clear that she wasn't going to make the call.

"Hello," she replied, careful to keep the tone of her voice neutral. She didn't stop walking.

"It's dangerous weather for a casual stroll, ma'am. Would you allow my, er, associate and I to give you a lift?"

"No, thanks." She barely spared him a glance, making sure she watched her step on the narrow and aging sidewalk. "I like the exercise. Besides, it's not far to the clinic."

"True, but what a shame it would be if our pretty, new doctor was the victim of a hit-and-run accident."

She'd been aware of his interest in her from the

moment he'd entered the clinic—Wade Maddox's manners were as coarse as his features—but Rachel had experienced her share of trouble with his kind before. By no means would she make the mistake of underestimating him, but she knew his interest would run out all the faster if she bored him with the formal civility that all Gentrys were indoctrinated in from birth.

"I stay on the sidewalk and close to the guardrail, Mr. Maddox, but thank you for your concern."

She'd hoped it would be enough to send him on his way. She was wrong. To her dismay, after a short exchange between the men inside, the car continued to keep pace beside her.

"Okay, I've got another idea. How about if we stop by the café and you let me buy you a cup of coffee— or better yet, a late breakfast?"

The mention of food made Rachel's normally healthy appetite resurface for the first time since she'd fled Jewel's disconcerting presence, but she knew she wouldn't be able to swallow a bite if Wade Maddox sat staring across the table at her.

"I'm afraid I don't have the time right now."

"Why not? I thought you said you worked the evening shift?"

"I do, but I have to...consult with Dr. Voss over a case. It's quite important."

"Sounds like a person needs to be sick or something to get near you."

"Yes, I'm afraid I stay very busy, Mr. Maddox."

"The least you can do is call me Wade."

She would rather deal with nightmares about Jay Barnes for the rest of her life and brood over Joe Becket. "How's your...how's Mr. Lawson doing?"

she asked, thinking that changing the subject might give him a subtle hint.

"Uh...as a matter of fact, I don't rightly know. Last I saw him, he was, um, moving on and thinking about seeking another form of employment."

Something about his sly reply, along with the driver's muffled guffaw, grated on Rachel. "I see. And just what is it that you do?"

"Oh, you might say I'm a...consultant. Yeah, that's it. I'm a consultant for a...a pest control firm."

This time the driver burst into outright laughter and hit the accelerator. As the car sped away, Rachel saw Wade Maddox punch the driver in the arm, then he stuck his head out the window and sent her a jaunty salute.

Feeling a chill that contradicted the sultry weather, Rachel stopped. She wanted to do everything she could to help the car get out of sight as fast as possible.

Rubbing her bare arms, she looked around. Right now, she mused, Joe Becket's presence would almost be a point of sanity in a very disturbing world. But there was no sign of him, nothing except the depressing mantle of fog.

With a sigh, she continued across the bridge.

CHAPTER EIGHT

The clinic was quiet when she entered through the reception area. Because she rarely came in at this hour, the quiet surprised her, but she found it a relief, too. It should, she reasoned, make it easier to ask Sammy for a few minutes of his time.

She was immediately glad she'd come. From the day she'd first arrived in Nooton, she'd felt as though she belonged here, as though she'd stepped into a safe zone. However, before she could enjoy the reassuring vibes too much, Cassie, the day receptionist, returned to her desk.

The can of diet soda the young woman had been in the process of popping open made an anticlimactic fizz as she gave Rachel a perplexed smile. "Hi. What are you doing here? You're not due in for—" she checked her watch "—good grief, hours. What's wrong?"

"Does something have to be wrong for me to come by early?" Rachel replied, affecting an incredulous laugh.

Cassie shrugged. "To each his own, I guess. You do look a bit strung out, though. You're not coming down with a bug, are you?" She was one of those unlucky souls who caught everything that came through the office, and had the faded-photograph type of face to prove it. It didn't surprise Rachel to see her put down her soft drink and cross her index fingers as though warding off a hex. "Please don't breathe on me. This is my first day back from a forty-eight-hour virus. I can't afford any more sick leave."

"Relax. I don't have anything contagious. Is Dr. Voss with a patient?" Rachel added, circling the desk to get to the hallway where their offices and the examination rooms were.

"He's finishing up with the last two that were scheduled for the morning. Unless we get an emergency, he should be available if you need to speak with him."

"I'll go wait in our office."

Rachel passed the file room and the children's examination room, remembering the first time she'd been escorted through the cramped but cozy building. The file cabinets were secondhand and no doubt had shown their wear even before Sammy purchased them, the decorations adorning the children's room were handmade by past and present staff, and the bulletin board outside the combination delivery-outpatient surgery room was growing crowded with photos of babies Sammy had assisted into the world. It all created an environment that managed to avoid the usual antiseptic, impersonal atmosphere other health-care facilities exuded. In fact, this one felt more like home than her room at Adorabella's, which made it much easier for Rachel to maintain her challenging schedule.

Officially, from four in the afternoooon—although she often came in at two or three—until two in the morning, the clinic served as the center of her life. Maybe that was the other reason she'd come here this morning, she mused, pausing by the photos. Maybe she'd wanted a reassurance that her world wasn't being completely shifted off its axis.

Marion, one of the two day nurses, came out of an examination room, spotted her and quickly shut the door behind herself. "I'm not sure you want to be here," she whispered to Rachel, tucking a pencil into her casual, more salt than pepper topknot.

Immediately sensing the tenseness in the tall woman, Rachel grew more wary. "What's up?"

"Cleo phoned earlier. She said she'd been up all night wrestling with her decision, but decided she had to go with her conscience. She reported that you closed the clinic early last night."

Rachel felt a lead weight descend on her chest. "I thought she might."

"She said you've been acting *bookoo* weird," the ex-triage nurse added, as usual peppering her dialogue with Vietnamese slang.

"I assume Sammy's vital signs are shaky?"

"You can say that again. Prepare yourself to hear the Gospel according to Voss. What in the world possessed you, hon?"

"Oddly enough, 'possessed' is quite appropriate phrasing, Marion, but I can't go into any explanations yet."

"Whatever it was, I hope it was worth it." She patted Rachel's shoulder. "Does it still look like doom and gloom outside?"

"Pretty much."

Marion shuddered. "Creepy stuff. You know what was on TV last night? *The Fog*. Naturally, my kid had to watch. Have you seen it? Whenever the stuff rolls in, these phantom pirates come back to a modern town to exact revenge for some treasure that was stolen from them."

"I remember," Rachel replied, attempting an

amused smile, although not quite succeeding. "One of my college roommates was addicted to stuff like that." She herself wouldn't have made the connection between the weather and the film, but now that Marion had brought it up, the parallel made her imagination kick into gear again.

Preoccupied, she didn't realize the nurse was frowning and reaching for her forehead until it was too late. Belatedly, she backed away.

"You're a little warm, Doctor. Maybe you'd better sit down," Marion said, tilting her head toward the office Rachel shared with Sammy. "Put your feet up and I'll tell him you're here."

Rather than argue that she was fine, Rachel did as Marion suggested. She needed to think about what Cleo had done, anyway.

She understood, of course, and bore no resentment toward the nurse. In fact, if their situations were reversed, she would probably have reacted the same way. Nevertheless, it complicated things; she just wouldn't be able to tell how much until she saw Sammy.

Their office was as cramped as the rest of the place, due to the two desks that were scrunched together along the far wall; the two steel-and-vinyl guest conference chairs for patient consultations were placed beside them, and the rest of the space was taken up by the inevitable file cabinets.

Rachel perched on the edge of her cleared desk and managed a crooked smile at the disaster scattered across Sammy's, which reflected the lively, emotional bachelor and pack rat behind the professional. Every afternoon when she came in, Rachel had to spend the first few minutes sweeping the overflow of material spilling onto her desk back over to his side. Here it was, barely 10:00 a.m., and already several pieces of mail and a stack of files were shoving her pen and pencil set across her blotter. She needed to sic Helga on him.

Helga was Sammy's live-in German housekeeper, who also cared for his elderly father. Originally hired over a year ago as a private nurse after Mr. Voss's stroke, she'd broadened her duties by her own choice because she couldn't believe anyone as unorganized as Sammy could function for long without help.

Rachel had a hunch Sammy was infatuated with the young woman, but saw himself as too old or too staid for her. Or maybe he was afraid that if he did lower the employer-employee barrier between them and things didn't work out, he would lose a trusted and valued helper.

The problem with the world, she concluded, comparing his situation with her own rather empty private life, was that there wasn't enough romance in it. Small wonder that the first man to have roused her curiosity in ages happened to be a ghost.

"Wouldn't Freud have fun with you," she muttered back to herself.

"This is not reassuring. The wunderkind is not supposed to be talking to herself."

Leave it to Sammy to sneak up on her, Rachel thought, shifting to find him in the doorway. She forced a bright smile. "I usually do, you know that."

"Mmm. But it's what you're saying that's disturbing." He stepped farther into the room and shut the door behind himself before rounding the desks to sit down in his chair.

Dr. Samuel Voss was a middle-aged man with coal-black hair that was trying to turn a distinguished gray at the sides, but instead looked as though it had paint streaks in it. Bland, slightly rounded features made his probing brown eyes more interesting and his kind mouth reassuring. But today the eyes had a harder glint to them and the mouth's corners were turned downward.

"You look like hell, kiddo," he announced, his New York accent still pronounced despite having lived in Nooton for twenty years.

"Good morning to you, too."

He folded his hands across his slight paunch. "Cute I don't need this morning. What I need is an explanation as to why you're doing your best to run yourself into the ground, and taking this clinic with you."

Preparing for battle, Rachel twisted her legs into a lotus position. The rebuke was nothing less than she deserved, but that didn't make it any easier to take. "You know better than that, Sammy."

"Do I? I thought I did. I trusted you because you seemed to share my own sense of responsibility to an ideal. Instead, I learn that last night you shut this place down well before the scheduled hour?"

"I know I went against policy, but nothing was happening."

"How would you know? You weren't here."

Guilt crushed down on her chest and shoulders, along with dread. "Did something happen?" She would never forgive herself if anything had. Even though she knew she'd been wrong to break the clinic's rules, she'd done so only when she'd been confident that they wouldn't be depriving anyone of emergency medical care. The boardinghouse's phone number, as well as Sammy's, was listed on the front door, further assuring that.

"All right, so there was no crisis, but that's not the point," he replied, scowling harder. "The point is something *could* have happened, and we both would have had to live with the consequences. What needs to be discussed is why? You came here with the same attitude I did when I opened the place. You said you wanted to help those who normally get shortchanged by the system. But from what I've learned from Cleo—and please don't hold this against her, because her motives were concern, not vindictiveness—lately you can't wait to get out of here. What's more, you're preoccupied. Troubled. Even I noticed that yesterday. It doesn't take second sight to see something's wrong. So now I'm asking. What's happened? I depend on you, Rachel. At home I have a father who's beginning to see people, family, who've been dead for years, including my mother. Let me tell you, with that pressure I don't need things to fall apart here."

Rachel bowed her head and considered her clenched hands. She'd come here with the express intention of telling him everything, but now she realized she couldn't do it. Not after this. If she tried to tell him that the reason she'd been closing early was to meet with a ghost on Black Water Creek Bridge, he would explode, maybe even have her shipped to Baton Rouge for psychiatric observation. Next he would notify her family, and then... Oh, God. She couldn't. She wouldn't do it. As open-minded as Sammy could be, this clearly wasn't a good time for him to deal with this. There had to be another way.

Even so, she owed him more than her cautious silence.

She took a breath, but couldn't think of anything to say. "It's complicated," she said, lifting her shoulders in a shrug to mirror the one he often gave her.

He recognized it and narrowed his eyes. "Stop that. And take your time."

Uh-huh, she thought. As long as it was the truth. That was the message in his eyes. "The truth is, I can't explain. Yet."

His heavy eyebrows angled into dark arrows. "Do you hear what you're saying? This is worse than I thought."

"Can you be patient with me for a while longer?"

"Patience is no problem. Negligence is another story, and I would be negligent if I didn't press you for more. You don't seem yourself, Rachel."

Wagging fingers now. It was all she needed. "No one is up to par these days with the weather as humid and depressing as it is," she cried.

"Maybe, but not to the point where they put a job on the line that they've trained almost half their life for."

A horrible thought crossed her mind. The sense of humor she was trying to maintain splintered. Died. "Sam...are you kicking me out?"

"I'm angry and disappointed, not demented. But you're not getting away with that nonsense about the weather, either." He scowled at the mess on his desk, but in a way that made her believe he didn't see any of it. Suddenly, he snapped his fingers. "It's the old hag, isn't it?"

"What? Who? Adorabella? She hasn't—"

"No, no. The other one. The quack too many people around here still use first before coming to me.

What's she done—threatened you with some kind of hocus-pocus swami business?''

"Of course not. Granted, she's strange..."

"The woman is a walking menace. First thing this morning I had a patient in here with an ulcerous stomach. Ulcers, for crying out loud—and between you and me, one meeting with her worthless husband and I could see how she got them. Then there's the five babies, two still in diapers... To top it all off, the bum's sniffing around her younger sister. Do you know what that crazy woman's advice to the poor soul was?''

Rachel could imagine and thought of the stories *she* could tell him. "But if you saw how protective Jewel is of Adorabella. I talked to her only a while ago, Sammy, and—"

"Eat a turtle heart," he continued as though she hadn't spoken. "Eat a *live* turtle's heart, she tells my patient. That's supposed to drive the bum out of her life and cure her problems." With a groan, he sat back in his chair and rubbed his hands over his face.

"You're the one who told me that we can't expect to alter people's beliefs overnight," Rachel reminded him, bending to get into his line of vision.

He gave her a warning look. "The reason I told you all that is so you'd understand I've heard it all. So, now out with it. What's the problem?"

Go ahead, ask him. Say, "Okay, Samuel, since we're on the subject of ghosts, turtle hearts and whatnot, let me tell you about the dead man I've met on Black Water Creek Bridge. I guarantee it'll finish turning your hair gray."

She moistened her lips. She racked her brain to think of a way to tell him. But in the end she could only shake her head. "I'm sorry. I need to handle this on my own."

Sammy sat forward and rested his hands on the paper-strewn blotter. "Do you hear what you're saying, Rachel? Do you know what you're forcing me—no, *inviting* me—to do?"

"I'm afraid so," she whispered.

CHAPTER NINE

"*You leave me no choice. I'm putting you on probation, effective immediately.*"

Rachel stood outside the clinic, weak-kneed from disbelief and miserably hurt, yet unable to cry. She'd long ago lost her ability to do that, back when she'd lost Roddie, but she was overwhelmed with a debilitating depression that was unlike anything she'd known since that horrible day.

"*You've hit a psychological wall, Rachel.*"

"*You've been carrying too heavy a load for too long, Rachel.*"

"*You're out...you're out...you're out...*"

What was she going to do? Besides the guilt of having failed Sammy—everyone—what was she going to do? She had bills to pay.

"*Until you've straightened things out and are ready to talk, I don't want to see you here.*"

Straighten things out. There was a joke. How could she do that when she didn't even know what was going on? But she knew that arguing with Sammy would have been useless. He'd been resolute, overwhelmed with his own problems. Even when she'd challenged him about the workload this would burden him with, he'd insisted he couldn't let it matter. He would solve the situation by working a few more hours each day, he'd told her, and close down for the rest as he'd done before she'd come to Nooton.

That had made her feel worse. She realized she

wasn't only letting him and the staff down, but the entire town.

Dejected, she walked across the parking lot. Two pickup trucks pulled into Alma's Country Cookin', reminding her that she hadn't eaten yet. She couldn't now. Whatever appetite she'd had was gone. It didn't help that she felt as though everyone inside was staring at her as she passed. She was almost relieved to get on the bridge and merge with the denser mist, despite its being the source of all her problems. Veering from her usual path, she walked on the right side this time, the side where she'd been seeing Joe. As she approached the spot, her heart began pounding harder. If ever she needed the reassurance that she hadn't been imagining all this, it was now. But what if he did appear? The mist wasn't anything like the denser nebula it became at night; would it be enough to hide her from the curious at the café, or the boardinghouse...or Beauchamp's? Doubtful, but despairing, she stopped, aware of her body's tension and her senses' alertness.

"Joe?" She clutched at the guardrail and looked beyond it, then below to the creek that was barely visible in the vaporous mix. "Are you there?" she called in a hushed voice.

She listened, waited, hoped...but in vain.

Of course he wasn't there. She stepped back from the railing both physically and mentally, and shoved her hands into the front pockets of her jeans. He wasn't there because, as Sammy had pointed out, she'd run headlong into a psychological wall as a result of the pressure she'd been under these past years. What if Joe was, indeed, a result of that stress overload? It was feasible. For all she knew, Jay Barnes's eccentricity could have played on her subconscious until she'd invented an alter ego of sorts, someone who intrigued her sexually and intellectually, yet was unattainable. Safe.

So deep was she in her self-analysis, that the phantomlike touch of a finger across her cheek had her jerking backward and up against a steel beam. Astonished, openly afraid, she looked around for whoever could have crept up on her without her hearing them.

But no one else was around.

Rachel lifted her hand to her cheek, wishing... afraid to wish.

"Then help me!" she cried out, spinning around in the direction from which she'd felt the touch, *his* touch. "Tell me what to do! Tell me why this is happening? Why *me?*"

Her only reply was the distant horn from the 10:35 out of Baton Rouge as it dragged itself through town like an armored centipede. The horn sounded again to warn vehicles and pedestrians of its approach to the Cotton Road crossing a half mile beyond the woods which blocked her view—if she'd been looking in that direction. She wasn't. She was staring at the man standing just outside of Beauchamp's garage.

How long had he been watching her? She could barely make him out in the concealing mist, let alone recognize him. But his typical uniform of jeans and T-shirt, and that hint of white on his hand, gave him away as much as his negative body language.

"What is it you know?" she murmured. This involved him somehow, and she was going to find out how. Because she suddenly had nothing but time on her hands, she was going to make sure of it.

Determined, she continued her walk across the

bridge. There must have been something in her step that got through to him because he seemed to grow more tense. Then, abruptly, he retreated back into the garage. Go ahead, she thought, try to hide. But this time there was no door to shut her out.

She walked briskly past the turn-off to the boardinghouse, along the gravel-strewn shoulder of the road, thinking about what she should say to him. If the dubiously named "Mudcat" Beauchamp was around, it would make things more difficult, maybe impossible. Somehow, though, she would figure out a way not to leave until Jay Barnes understood she had things to say to him.

Beauchamp's was one of those places her mother would have described as "men's territory," an environment no refined woman would be caught in. The smell of petroleum products, sweat and whatever had been discarded in the fifty-gallon oil drums on each of the two fuel-pump islands assaulted her nostrils when she was still a dozen or so yards from the brown sheet-metal building. Rachel decided this area could give some hospital odors a legitimate challenge.

She spotted Dwight Beauchamp through the glass door of his office. Even though he saw her, too, and held up a fat finger, obviously meant to signal "I'll be with you shortly," she pretended she didn't notice and continued inside.

Jay Barnes stood at the back wall of the garage, partially hidden by a large truck, the kind that transported the crude oil from the wells on the south part of town to the refinery in Baton Rouge. He seemed to be trying to dismantle some kind of spray gun; however, due to his injured hand, he was having problems.

Although the thick rubber soles of her athletic shoes made virtually no sound on the cement, she could tell from his squared shoulders and stiff bearing that he knew she'd arrived. It made it easier to think of an opening line.

"How's the hand today?"

"Not bad enough to warrant a house call."

"This isn't a professional visit. I simply found myself in the area and thought it would be polite to ask."

He set the spray gun onto the wooden workbench hard enough to rattle a number of the cans and tools scattered across it and turned around. "You put great stock in being polite, do you?"

His deep voice turned silky smooth, which had Rachel debating exactly how much bolder she should get during this confrontation. She decided that, no matter what, direct was best. "Why are you working so hard at intimidating me?"

"Because I want you to leave me alone."

"Believe me, the feeling's mutual."

That seemed to give him a moment's pause. Then he crossed his arms, and she found herself staring at muscles that said he wasn't a man used to laying around and watching TV.

"You're good, I'll give you that," he muttered. "Playing the dedicated professional with just the right amount of innocence mixed in to emphasize your femininity."

Rachel hated hearing herself reduced to the bare essentials like a microwave cupcake. She shoved her hands deeper into her pockets to keep herself from taking a not-too-smart swing at him. Roddie had always said she should have been born a boy for all her tomboyish impulses. "It's not going to work, you know. This macho technique of trying to scare me into minding my own business is...bunk. I may not have the investigative skills to find out why you're treating me like this, but I have my own reasons for trying."

"And what might they be?" Jay Barnes replied in a tone that indicated he wouldn't believe her, no matter what she said.

Rachel wished she could afford to wet her lips, but she didn't want to give him the satisfaction of knowing how his steady stare intimidated her. "I've seen you before. No, to be more accurate, someone who looks like you. Too much like you not to be related. Only he didn't call himself Barnes...but his initials *were* J.B."

Was it concern over job security or something else that had him shooting a glance toward the office to see if she'd been overheard? Rachel felt her heartbeat kick into overdrive. Had she pushed too hard? What if he tried something here?

After another long moment of studying her, he said, "If you know what's good for you, you'll get out of here. Now."

"You haven't answered my question."

"And I don't intend to."

"Then I'm staying."

He took a step toward her. "Do you know all I have to do is turn on one of those compressors over there and it would make enough of a racket to block out almost any sound you might make?"

"Trying to bully me again, Mr. Barnes?"

"Glad you're bright enough to pick up on that."

Rachel searched his hard, uncompromising face, the bottomless pools of his unreadable eyes, and wondered how far she dared go before she had to retreat. "What's the plan? Murder? Rape?"

"I'm feeling generous. Pick one."

When he took another step toward her, she decided it was time to step back. "Maybe I should warn you that I'm stronger than I look."

"Sure you are."

The next step was pure reflex. "If you are foolish enough to try anything, you won't get away with it."

"Oh, I bet I would. But on the other hand, what makes you think I care at this point?"

The back of her thighs came in abrupt contact with the truck's front fender. It had a crushing effect on her bravado. "Stop it," she whispered.

"I will…if you'll get lost."

"Talk to me first."

"About what?"

"You. Who are you?"

"Jay Barnes."

"That's a lie." Rachel couldn't believe the words came from her mouth, but once they did, she knew there was no taking them back. And somehow she didn't want to. As for Jay Barnes, he looked ready to pounce.

"What did you say?"

His voice held that familiar deceptive softness and Rachel was more than a little relieved to hear the office door open and Dwight Beauchamp call, "What's up, J.B.?"

Hearing those initials, Rachel stared up at the man who, out of sight of his boss, had her wrist in a painful grasp. She had the oddest feeling that he hadn't even heard the man. "Let me go," she demanded, her lips frozen from contained fear.

"Shut up." He glanced around the truck toward Beauchamp and called, "Nothing."

"Lady need some bodywork done?"

Rachel suffered Jay Barnes's insolent gaze sweeping down her body. It left her feeling as though she'd been undressed and more.

"Not hardly."

"Say what?"

"She's my neighbor," he said more loudly. "She's, uh, returning something I'd dropped."

Mudcat made a sound of disappointment. "Well, don't forget you've gotta get that paint job done." Then he retreated into his office and once again slammed the door behind him.

Rachel wanted to shout for him to stay. But the pain in her wrist intensified, letting her know what a mistake it would be.

"I'll give you one last chance," Jay Barnes growled over the echo of the shuddering wood and glass. "If you're the innocent you claim to be, get out of here."

"All right. All *right*," she cried, jerking her hand free. As soon as she was able, she sidestepped him and backed toward the street. "You win. For now."

"What the hell is that supposed to mean?"

"*You* worry about it."

CHAPTER TEN

Not wanting to give him the chance to get near her again, Rachel ran out of the garage and into the welcome grayness. She didn't slow her hurried pace until she reached the dirt road and saw he wasn't following her. But her thoughts continued racing.

If she couldn't get any answers from Jay Barnes, she would try another way. One option remained viable. She didn't relish the idea of doing it, but at this rate she didn't see that she had a choice. Somehow she had to get into his room.

She expected obstacles—upstairs. What she didn't expect was running into the first one the moment she reached the boardinghouse.

Contrary to what Jewel had anticipated, the old woman was up and dressed. As Rachel entered, Adorabella floated from parlor to foyer looking much like one of the spirits she insisted shared the house with them.

As with all her outfits, her dress was ankle length to hide, as she put it, her bean-pole legs. The pink silk chenille clashed somewhat with lavender hair styled in wispy waves that competed with the frills at her collar and wrists. How she managed to keep her frail body balanced in her strappy pumps baffled Rachel, even if the shoes only had two-inch heels. Both Jewel and Sammy often pleaded with her to respect her age and her frailty, but Adorabella insisted her feet were her vanity and she would show them to an advantage as long as they suited her. She did use a silver-handled cane that, when not saving her neck, was used like a schoolteacher's pointer. Rachel found herself at the end of its sterling tip the moment she shut the screen door.

"There you are!" Adorabella cried, her rice-paper cheeks flushed by excitement and rouge. "Come look at what they've done this time. I'm so glad you're back. I wanted another witness, but when I heard you'd gone out, I thought, 'What am I to do now?' Mr. Bernard is with his fogies and I'm afraid to ask if Celia's dragged herself back yet. Of course, Jewel can't count, you know. She's got the power. People would say it was all her doing."

Rachel cast a yearning glance toward the stairs. "Look at what?" she forced herself to ask, knowing instinctively that she didn't want to hear any more, and she certainly didn't want to get involved.

"Come, come, come. It'll do no good just telling you. We're going to take a picture, too. That is, as soon as Jewel gets back with some film for the camera. We've decided to send the photo to the Nooton *Gazette*. Last time I had a message from the other side, that smart-alecky editor in chief over there told me to get him a photograph. I'm going to see he gets one this time. I'll prove they're here, once and for all."

"Adorabella," Rachel said, continuing to linger behind, "I really do need to go up and—"

Her landlady rapped her cane on the wooden floor twice. "Don't dawdle, Rachel."

Aware she wouldn't get away until she'd obliged her, Rachel followed. But with a sinking feeling. She remembered only too well the last "encounter" she'd

witnessed on behalf of Adorabella. All the portraits
and photos in the parlor had been askew, and the
glasses around the liqueur decanter were turned on
their sides. One had still been rolling back and forth.

"You just missed them," Adorabella had whispered.

Rachel had been amused. She'd also never thought
anything about repercussions when she'd added her
signature as witness to the statement Adorabella had
Jewel write. She'd been under the impression it was
simply something for their personal album of mem-
oirs. Later, however, when the reporter from the *Gazette* stopped by the clinic—*after* researching her
background enough to see newsworthiness in a story
about a Gentry in Nooton—the idea of allowing
Adorabella her fun rapidly grew less innocent or
harmless.

"All right, I'm coming," she sighed, preparing
herself for the worst. "But I'm warning you up front,
I won't sign anything, and I'm not giving any inter-
views, either."

"No need, no need. That's why we're taking the
photograph."

Before Rachel could ask why they needed her then,
the old woman tapped her way through the parlor to
the dining room. Rachel brought up the rear. One
minute, she told herself, then no matter what, she
would return to her own agenda.

Adorabella stopped in the entryway of the dining
room and posed, her cane thrust toward the table.
"Now, what do you make of *that?*" she demanded,
her frail voice lowered dramatically.

Rachel considered the crystal vase that a few hours
ago had contained the huge bouquet of roses. All the

blossoms were now scattered around the tablecloth, and most were petalless.

"Well?" Adorabella asked, sounding more proud than upset. "Don't you think this will convince them?"

Rachel eyed her landlady before looking back at the mess. "Are you alleging that the spirits of the house did this, too?"

"Who else?"

Clearing her throat, Rachel reasoned, "The blossoms were almost dead, Adorabella." She didn't want to hurt her feelings. When the old woman got depressed, she had a tendency to get even more reckless with the pills and liquor. "They could have fallen off naturally."

"The stems, dear, look at the stems. Some of them are out, too."

She had a point there. "I don't suppose someone happened to see this happening?" she asked hopefully.

"Of course not. That's the whole point," Adorabella declared, accenting the last two words by beating her cane on the carpeted floor. "Jewel and I were in the kitchen and no one else was around. But don't you see what's most fascinating? No, of course you don't, because you're not standing in the best place. Come over here."

The woman took hold of her arm and led her to the side of the table. Releasing Rachel, she pointed to the right side of the vase. "See?"

Even as she told herself it was an illusion, Rachel stared at the *J* spelled awkwardly with the rose stems. She blinked hard, but the image remained.

"My beloved husband's name was Justin. I've

been trying to contact him for over twenty years. He died up in the room Celia is renting, but we'll keep that our little secret, if you please. No need to upset her. Of course, I was angry with Justin for the longest time for not chasing her out of there, but maybe this is his way of making up for it. Isn't it clever of him to use his favorite flower to get a message to me? And look…he even used the petals to make a heart and let me know he still loves me. He always was such a romantic man."

The petals were indeed more organized after the crooked *J*, but Rachel didn't see a heart as Adorabella did. She saw a lower-case *o. J-o.* A cold chill raced down her spine. No, she thought, it couldn't be.

Joe?

"Got it!" Jewel rushed in from the kitchen, an Instamatic camera in hand. When she looked up from locking in the film cartridge and saw Rachel, there was a brief flicker in her dark eyes before she asked Adorabella, "How do you want this?"

Ever the born director, her landlady prodded Rachel along. "Rachel and I will stand at the opposite side of the table and you stay there to get in the writing."

The farce had gone on long enough. Rachel hung back, shaking her head. "I'm sorry. I can't participate in this." She began edging out of the room.

"Nonsense. One picture, that's all." Adorabella hooked Rachel's arm with her cane.

Short of creating a scene and rousing unwanted curiosity, there seemed to be no way out of it. Rachel relented, but as she faced the camera, unsmiling, it also crossed her mind that she would be wise to placate Adorabella, especially when she didn't have a

clue as to how long she would be out of work, and
that she might have to ask for a few days' extension
on the rent.

At the first opportunity, she made her excuses and
began to withdraw.

Jewel followed her to the stairs. "Be careful," she
said, her voice vibrating with ominous warning.

Not certain whether she was being warned or
threatened, Rachel's heart made a faint lurch. "What
do you mean?"

"You and I both know it wasn't Mr. Justin who
left that message. It was put there for you."

As much as she yearned to put a great deal of distance between herself and the woman, Rachel also
saw the need to appear calm and confident. "Do we?
For all we know, it's a message to the widow of Jack
Bonnard."

She was grateful to see she'd scored a point with
that, but Jewel recovered quickly and shook her turbaned head.

"Seen you talking to *him*." She nodded in the direction of Beauchamp's. "You look hard enough for
trouble, Doctor, you'll find it. That's what the spirits
be saying."

"I was merely checking on Mr. Barnes's hand.
He'd hurt it yesterday and I bandaged it for him last
night," she explained when the woman failed to make
any comment. Then she experienced a flash of per-
ception. "Wait a minute. No ghost was responsible
for those roses, *you* were. Why? To scare me into
taking you seriously?"

The older woman muttered something in a language Rachel didn't understand. "Believe what you

want," she replied darkly. "But don't say I didn't warn you."

Rachel waited until Jewel disappeared back into the dining room before continuing upstairs. The woman was a case for the books, all right, she thought with a sigh. But added to the events of the past few days, along with Sammy's decision to put her on probation, she didn't need this.

The events of the morning were taking their toll on her. Her head was spinning and her nerves felt as though they'd been put through a tenderizer.

All the more reason to resolve the mystery surrounding Jay Barnes and Joe Becket.

Once in her room, she set to work looking for something she could use to unlock her neighbor's door. The hardware, she decided while eyeing it across the hall, was old. A small screwdriver or hairpin might do the trick with the lock, except that she owned neither—and she wasn't about to go downstairs and borrow anything. Which left what?

C'mon, Gentry. You've seen plenty of whodunits and thrillers to have learned something.

She snapped her fingers. How obvious!

Hurrying back to the dresser, she grabbed her purse, pulled out her wallet and flipped through her credit cards. Which could she sacrifice in case the experiment didn't work? She didn't charge anything these days, because she simply couldn't afford to, but she'd held on to the major bankcards in case of an emergency. After a moment, however, it struck her that the raised digits and letters on each card might create a problem. She needed something shaped like this, but completely flat.

The bottom card was her driver's license. Ideal, she thought and dashed across the hall to try it out.

It amazed her how easily it worked. After only the second attempt, she heard a metallic clicking sound, and when she tried the knob, it yielded.

But her congratulatory mood quickly turned into concern. No matter how she looked at it, this was a criminal offense. "Miss Conscientious," as Roddie used to call her, although she knew he'd said it with pride rather than mockery, had become a common burglar. What would her brother, her idol, have had to say to that?

As she mentally browbeat herself, the door slowly swung open on its own, as though deciding for her. Nevertheless, she stayed where she was a moment longer, looking inside.

It was just four walls, a ceiling and a floor, she reminded herself. Nothing could harm her. And she'd come this far—she had to finish.

His room was no less bare than hers, or dull, she noted, grimacing at the tiny print wallpaper against a background of ash white. The bed was larger, she envied him that. But as for the rest—the bureau, a side table and a chair—she decided she wasn't the only one who'd chosen for location rather than atmosphere. All she had to figure out was why.

He had two views compared to her one: a window that looked out over the front yard, and beyond to Beauchamp's and the street, as well as one that matched her scan of the driveway and Black Water Creek. Was that significant? If so, it was also disturbing, since the only reason she could think of to warrant such a need was if someone was interested in keeping track of the comings and goings of people.

Rachel wandered from one side of the room to the other, her mind churning. What should she be looking for? Something—anything—that gave her more of a clue as to who he was.

There wasn't much to inspect, and searching the obvious—the closet, drawers—proved uninspiring. She'd thought *she* traveled light; Jay Barnes made her look like the original material girl. Most of the bureau drawers were bare, and when she checked the closet there was an empty canvas bag on the floor and a few pairs of jeans and a sports jacket on the hangers. Nothing suspicious. Nothing to identify him.

Rachel backed up to the bed and sat down. It didn't make sense. Even she had a few things lying around that at least characterized her to some degree…a favorite tortoiseshell brush from a friend here, a well-worn paperback version of an Ayn Rand novel there. Jay Barnes had virtually nothing, save a few old newspapers piled on the chair by the window. She should have guessed it would be like this, though. In the bathroom he kept a toothbrush, toothpaste, throwaway razor and mouthwash. Not even any aspirin, for heaven's sake, she thought, recalling how she'd once checked his side of the medicine cabinet. The man was practically invisible.

What did it mean? There was a lesson to be learned from this, just as there would be if he'd turned out to be the original human pack rat. It took her a moment to realize that, but once she did her interest and excitement grew. It also convinced her that there had to be something hidden somewhere. A man couldn't live here all these weeks and not be hiding something—unless he carried it on his person. Judging by Jay

Barnes's usual state of dress—or undress—that didn't seem likely.

So where had he stashed it? She drummed her fingers on the faded blue fitted sheet that was the only covering on the bed. Suddenly, she stopped and stared down. Obvious, yes, she told herself, but so had been the credit-card idea.

Sliding to the floor, she searched between the mattress and box spring, careful that when she withdrew her probing hands, she left the sheet and mattress cover as neat as she'd found it. But again there was nothing.

Rising, she checked behind the pillows and the headboard, and the single painting in the room, which was a faded watercolor of the bayou at dusk. None of those places proved any more helpful.

She peered behind each piece of furniture. Again it amazed her to see how little the man had with him. She'd seen transients newly arrived off one of the freight trains who carried more belongings.

"For heaven's sake," she muttered to herself once again in the closet. She slid to the floor and stared out at the room. He had to be hiding *something*.

It was chance alone that had her gaze settling on the bed again. No, that wasn't entirely true. She couldn't help imagining him lying there in the darkness, hot, naked and waiting for sleep—or dawn. It took her several seconds to realize she was staring at the slight unevenness of the box spring.

She sprang to her feet and sped across the room, sliding the last yard on her knees. Crouching low, she peered under the bed and saw it—the gun first...and then the billfold.

Knowing nothing about guns, and having a strong

aversion to the idea of learning, she left it alone and tugged the billfold free. Flipping it open, she immediately saw that it wasn't a billfold at all, but a leather identification...a policeman's ID.

She stared at the gold shield and then the laminated card bearing his picture. It was a terrible picture, but that wasn't what had her whispering, "Oh, my God."

The sound of the door shutting softly behind her might as well have been gunfire. She gasped and spun around.

"Lady," he growled, "it's time somebody taught you a lesson or two."

CHAPTER ELEVEN

"I told myself it wasn't possible," Rachel whispered, looking from Joe Becket's ID to the man glaring at her. "I know you look like him. Logic told me you had to be him. But he was so...different, so kind."

"What the hell are you talking about?" he snapped.

She almost laughed. "You wouldn't believe me if I told you."

"In that case, put that on the nightstand and move away from the bed. No tricks."

Instead, she continued to sit there, her body refusing to move, except to begin an involuntary trembling. "I can't."

"This isn't a bluff. Move."

"I...c-can't," she said, her teeth chattering. Reaction, she told herself. Too much happening in too short a time on too little food and rest. System overload. Psychic shock. "L-look, about breaking in...I know this looks b-bad."

"At least we agree on something."

"But I had my reasons."

"I never doubted it for a moment."

"What I'm t-trying to say is...this isn't what you think." It was probably worse. Even as that notion formed, Rachel struggled to rise to her knees; however, her bones felt like melting wax and the room was spinning crazily, leaving her nauseous. "Oh, God. This is too much to take in."

"You can cut the act. The game's over."

Indignation and anger boiled within her, a surprising but welcome antidote. "How can you be such a—?"

"Bastard? Easy. Watch someone you care about die sometime."

She had the strangest urge to laugh. It rose up her throat and she had to press her lips together and clench her hands into fists to keep it contained. But slowly she won the battle.

Finally, she was able to draw a shaky breath and reply, "Oh, but I have, Detective Becket. I have."

"Don't call me that."

"That's your name, isn't it?"

"I'll ask the questions…and I didn't mean in the course of your work."

"I see. Because it's not supposed to count when you're a professional? Well, you're wrong. It counts very much. Just as it counted when it was my brother, though technically he was already dead when I found his body. But the second time…the third and fourth times…oh, yes, I got to watch. That's why I'm in this mess."

He took a step toward her. "So, you are involved."

"Involved?" The word again reminded her that she was as confused about what she'd gotten herself caught up in, as he was about her. "Not in the way I think you mean."

"Liar!"

Her denial seemed to break through to some violent thing gestating inside him so that when he took another step toward her, her instinct was to retreat. She darted sideways, and her denim-clad legs scraped against the fitted sheet like fingernails assaulting a chalkboard. It was the echo of her fear, and a mistake.

His hands reached for her; she tried to evade. Bigger, faster, stronger, he won. But like a spring recoiling, the force of his movements sent her flying backward and threw him off balance, as well.

They fell onto the bed. For a lean man, he was built like a brick wall, solid and undefeatable. Overwhelmed by the full impact of his weight crushing her into the mattress, Rachel had her hands full struggling to breathe. Until all the fighting and writhing settled him solidly between her thighs and she became acutely, unignorably reminded that he was all male.

She didn't want to be aware, dreaded the shiver that betrayed her sensitivity to him. But as soon as her gaze was drawn to his and she found the fierce storm of his angry blue eyes altering, subduing, she reminded herself about *who* she was dealing with.

If she believed in what she'd experienced on the bridge.

If she could trust his ID.

If she rejected every piece of scientific data she'd been taught since undergraduate school.

Deciding she'd already made that decision the second night she'd crossed the bridge, she let herself relax and accept his weight, his superiority, his intimacy. She also forced herself to hold his affected, but stubbornly hard gaze with empathy and compassion in hers. Nothing, she was sure, like what he'd been expecting.

She felt the change in his body first, a twitch of an abdominal muscle, a tightening in his loins and groin. It didn't take a handful of degrees to recognize what was happening, but it allowed her to recognize he was definitely not as immune to her as he wanted it to appear.

"It won't work," he ground out.

"What won't?"

"The bravado or whatever the hell you're trying to achieve. It's a nice try, but I can tell you're afraid."

"Not any longer. Not about what you think."

"Then you're more of a fool than I thought possible."

"Maybe. But nothing you're liable to threaten me with will make it easier to break."

"*It?* What?"

"The ties that bind me to you."

Once again she felt an involuntary physical reaction, his body tightening, hardening against hers. In response, hers grew warmer, taut in places, and softer in others. On some level she knew it was insane, *wrong,* for her to be letting this happen. First and foremost, they were virtual strangers and, try as she might, she couldn't forget the social mores that insisted she should have some self-respect.

But she couldn't help herself. A stronger urge insisted she follow her hunch. What fascinated her, though, was learning that Jay or Joe, or whatever he wanted to call himself, didn't seem to have much control over his reaction to her, either.

What she wasn't prepared for was the moment he shifted his focus and stared at her mouth. Suddenly, she had a flashing glimpse of their future; in a fleeting instant of clarity, she understood why the Joe on the bridge had looked at her with such aching longing and—yes, she could admit it now—possession.

She was going to come to know this man as intimately, as thoroughly, as two people could. The shock of that realization sent shivers of excitement and helpless desire through her body.

"I wonder," he muttered, after a small eternity, "would you really do anything to save your pretty neck?"

"Does it matter? You won't hurt me."

Her quiet resolve seemed to fill him with more agitation. "Didn't anyone ever tell you it's sheer stupidity to play chicken with a desperate man?"

Yes, she'd heard such advice, quite a few times, actually. But it had no impact on her at the moment. As incredible a situation as this was, she couldn't forget that no matter how angry he might appear, she'd seen him first—on the bridge—without this mask of aggression...and she could never go back.

"You won't hurt me," she said again, with more confidence than she knew she should be feeling, "because at your core you're fair and decent. I may not have been sure of that before, and I'm afraid of *how* I know it now, but I do."

"What the hell are you talking about?"

"It's a long story. One I'm nowhere near finished with putting together myself. How can I begin to explain it to you?" As she spoke, she gazed wonderingly up into his face. It amazed her that she was growing increasingly calm with every second. Even as the lights in his eyes sharpened, grew flinty, Rachel understood and felt herself becoming entwined in his feelings, his fears...his reluctant desire for her.

"It's all right," she said, aware of the battle he waged within himself. "I'm no danger to you."

"In case you hadn't noticed, you're in the wrong

position to be reassuring. You need to be worrying about how much danger I am to *you*."

Only to her heart. The thought sent a shiver of trepidation through her; along with discovering Jay Barnes was Joe Becket, came the revelation of what such news had to mean.

"Damn it, stop looking at me that way!" he demanded, at once wary and yet tightening his grip on her wrists. When she didn't, he swore again and crushed his mouth to hers.

Rachel had been expecting this, and yet nothing could have prepared her for the unleashed power of it. She was almost oblivious to the pain of his hands biting into hers, his mouth as it moved relentlessly over hers. In a few brief moments, he swept away every preconception and experience she'd had regarding intimacy and desire. Only her heart remained sharply aware of how he resented succumbing to this.

The kiss went on and on, ruthless yet greedy. And his body...his body pressed her even deeper into the bedding, moved against her as though their clothes were inconsequential.

How was such passion possible so quickly? she wondered dizzily, as he angled his head to seek more of her. They were strangers. Yet she couldn't keep from wanting and responding to the wild abandon of his kiss any more than she could stop her body from accepting the powerful intrusion of his and challenging him to show her more.

A sound broke from him, one that resembled pain as well as denial. She heard it the same instant she tasted blood. That was why, when he tore his mouth from hers, she was unable to do more than fight to catch her breath.

Stunned and tortured expressions transformed his face like a series of splintering masks as he, too, struggled with his lost control. The sight of her dazed but accepting gaze seemed to flabbergast him; the smear of blood from her cut and swelling lip clearly shamed him.

"That's just a sample of how bad it's going to get if you don't start talking," he rasped.

All she could think to say was "How could you want me so much? How can I want you? It shouldn't be possible."

"I don't want you," he snapped.

"Yes, you do. You hate it, but you do." When she saw the glint of temper and the steely control that allowed him to drag himself off her and the bed, she knew she'd touched a deep nerve. "I meant what I said before. I'm not any danger to you. At least," she continued, sitting up and touching her lip, "not in the way you've been suspecting."

"Can it," he growled. "If you're intent on seeing something that isn't there, then that's your problem. But I promise you, you're not leaving this room until you tell me what I want to know."

Rachel might have almost believed he meant it, he managed to put that much icy disdain in his voice. However, he also made the mistake of shifting his gaze to her lip and quickly looking away. She attempted a faint smile. "It doesn't really hurt."

"Then I promise it will next time."

"No. From now on, you'll work even harder not to touch me."

"Don't count on it. Right now nothing would give me more pleasure than to wipe that smug smile off your face."

She wanted to clarify that her smile wasn't smug; instead she caught him touching his injured hand. Certain he must have hurt it again, she slid off the bed and went to help. As she reached for it, he backed away as though she was some venomous snake.

The brisk knock on the door kept her from trying again.

Rachel saw Joe stiffen and met his sharp look. From the other side of the door came Jewel's voice.

"Mr. Barnes? You in there?"

Rachel met Joe's stare. He looked as though he expected her to scream for help or something. Instead she lifted an eyebrow in query, which earned her a scowl. He then tilted his head toward the door.

Her hands shaking from the last few minutes of surging adrenalin, she released the lock and opened up. "Yes, Jewel? Is something the matter?"

Jewel stared at her mouth for a long moment before shooting an ominous look at Joe. "You okay?" she asked her.

There was no telling what the woman was thinking, and Rachel's mind was too full of other matters to try. "Of course. As I told you earlier, Mr....Mr. Barnes hurt his hand at work yesterday and I was about to change the bandage. Did you need me for something?"

"I just brought up fresh towels for the bathroom, and I saw your door open. Couldn't help being concerned," she added pointedly.

"That's very kind, but as you can see, I'm fine."

"Uh-huh." Jewel's gaze darted between them again. "Miss Adorabella also said to ask if you wanted to lunch with her before you went in to work?"

"As a matter of fact, I'm not, um, going in to the clinic. Dr. Voss has decided I need some time off."

Jewel nodded slowly, her expression unreadable. "In that case you'll be wanting to come down for dinner, too."

"Well, I'm not sure...."

"You taking time off, too?" Jewel demanded, turning to Joe.

"Maybe."

"Uh-huh. Lunch'll be ready in an hour. Dinner is at five-thirty. Come if you want to. Don't if you don't." She focused on Rachel's mouth once more. "Ain't any of my business."

As she began to turn away, Rachel touched her arm. "Jewel!"

The woman paused.

"Thank you."

After a slight hesitation, Jewel reached into her apron pocket and drew out the ball of black wax Rachel had left downstairs. "You forgot this."

She pressed it into Rachel's hand and shuffled off down the hallway. Boards creaked loudly under the weight of her heavy shoes. Rachel listened until she heard her start down the stairs, then hastily set the ball on the night table.

"You and the voodoo queen joining forces?" Joe drawled, easing between her and the door. He shut it with barely a sound.

"She's afraid you're trouble for me."

"That's like arsenic telling a .45 it's deadly."

Preoccupied with wondering how to dispose of the nasty-looking wax, Rachel turned to Joe in surprise when she heard the sound of the lock. "Didn't I just prove to you that I can be trusted?"

"Hardly. You didn't sound any more eager to explain yourself to her than I did. That only confirms I was right. You've got something to hide, and you're not leaving here until you tell me what it is."

She shut her eyes and shook her head. "You don't know what you're asking. It's not something I can casually blurt out to you. What's more, you're not going to believe me when I do tell you."

"Try me."

Rachel took a deep breath and shifted her hands to cover her queasy stomach. "I think... No, it's more than that. I *know* you're going to die."

CHAPTER TWELVE

"This may come as a shock to you, Doctor, but everybody kicks the bucket sooner or later," Joe said, grateful that he managed not to show any outward reaction. But inside he felt shaken to his core. How could he not when, from the moment she'd moved in, he'd been wondering if she was one of Garth's people sent to silence him, all the while knowing it did nothing to lessen his desire for her?

"By a gunshot wound to the stomach?"

His abdominal muscles tensed spasmodically. Of all the ways he'd imagined it happening—and in his line of work there were plenty—he tried not to think about that one. It ranked up on his list of dreads along with having to spend his life in a wheelchair or being reduced to a vegetable. But what disturbed him most was the certainty with which she spoke. "Do you know something I don't?"

Rachel bowed her head and massaged her shoulders. He was beginning to recognize the gesture as a habit performed when she was hot, restless...or nervous. Considering that she kept to herself almost as much as he did, he'd been storing up an abundant supply of trivia about her. And now that he knew what she tasted like, he realized he'd learned too much.

"I've been experiencing a strange phenomenon," Rachel told him, with a caution that matched the returning unease in her brown eyes.

If anything, those eyes were going to be his un-doing; wide and clear, with the slightest hint of a tilt at their corners, they possessed both an intelligence to be reckoned with and a softness born of an irre-sistible sensitivity. "Phenomenon?"

"Since Monday. Since the weather changed."

As he saw how her gaze seemed to be drawn to the side window that looked out toward Black Water Creek and the bridge, he let his follow. "The fog?"

"Not exactly. It's what's in it."

"Something's *in* it?"

"Try to remember that you're the one who asked," she shot back, her tone defensive. But once she turned back to the window she grew apologetic again. "And I suppose because it involves you, you deserve to be told. Only..." Once again she reached up to her shoulder.

"Will you cut that out," Joe muttered, frustrated because he'd been thinking how he would like to brush her hand aside and press his lips there.

"What did I do?"

Feeling like an idiot, he said, "Just stop fidgeting and finish what you were saying."

She nodded, but continued to look confused over his outburst. "All right. But please understand, until this happened, I wasn't the type to give credence to the, um, paranormal."

What the hell...? He wanted to laugh. He almost swore. Crushing both impulses, he thought, no. He wouldn't say anything. Let her finish trying to play him for a fool and see what happened.

"On Monday," she began, using the low, quiet voice he'd found himself listening for when they were both in the house, "when we closed the clinic, I had to walk home because the woman who usually gives me a lift back here—had car problems.''

She'd said here, not home; Joe filed away the small tidbit of information, which raised dozens of other questions. ''Why don't you have a car?''

''I sold it to pay bills. My college loans, to be exact.''

''Give me a break.'' This was obviously going to be a bigger trial on his patience than he'd first thought.

''Why not? It was worth more than what I'll earn in two years working here, plus it retired a hefty chunk of my tuition debt.''

''That's not what I was commenting on. I was referring to someone with your background insinuating you've had it tough. Don't forget, the Duchess is a diehard gossip. She told me who your old man is.''

''Maybe if you'd listened longer, you'd have learned I'm also the black sheep in my family,'' she retorted, a hint of gold fire in her eyes. ''I turned down their offer to pay for my education in order to choose my own school, my own career *and* the right to live my life on my own terms.''

''Honey, no one in their right mind spends the small fortune you must have to get your degree and *volunteers* to come to this slug capital of Louisiana.''

''The loan program I was part of had a moral commitment clause,'' she explained, with a dignity he had to admire. ''The basic concept is that you get your tuition, but upon graduation you've agreed to serve two years at a location that ordinarily can't afford decent medical staffing.''

''Sounds as though you'd have to be a saint or a fool to agree to something like that.'' Once again her eyes turned bright with temper, and Joe grimaced. "Okay, okay. Finish."

"Forget it."

She spun away from him and he caught her by the upper arm. *"Finish."*

What was it about her that tied him in knots so easily? From the first time he saw her walking to work with the midafternoon sun highlighting the russet and gold in her squeaky-clean hair and her filly-slim body moving with the grace of a woman totally at ease with herself, he'd been living for the next glimpse of her. Even in the bathroom, he searched for a hint of her presence—the scent of her soap or body lotion. On nights when he was too hot or edgy to sleep, he went to the window and listened for the low, not-quite-on-key humming that drifted over from her window, telling him that she'd come in from work and found it as impossible to settle down as he did.

Yes, he hated wanting her. If the day came when she realized how fast and thoroughly his craving for her had grabbed hold, it would give her a power that could destroy him. But he didn't know how to shut it off. More accurately, the harder he tried the less he succeeded.

"Finish," he said thickly.

Did she see the internal war he was waging with himself? Whatever the reason, she seemed to relax. Relieved, Joe withdrew his hand. She appeared grateful, too, and retreated to the far side of the bed where she leaned against the window frame. But even that distance wasn't far enough for him to ignore the droplets of moisture pooling at the hollow of her throat, or the debilitating impulse he felt to absorb that liquid with his lips and tongue.

"I walked," she said again. She crossed her arms beneath her firm breasts. "The town was more quiet than usual. The lounge had already closed and most of the traffic was gone. No doubt the weather had something to do with that, since the mist had already settled in. You might recall it started moving in around nightfall. I remember taking a coffee break and watching it descend almost in slow motion."

"You can skip the melodrama. I don't spook easily."

"I used to say the same thing," she replied, casting him a look he almost believed was sympathetic. Then she refocused on the view out the window. "As I began across the bridge, the mist grew so dense, it seeped through my clothes and clung to my skin. I could barely see two steps in front of me. And that's when I heard it. I'll never forget it as long as I live."

"Heard what?"

"A man's gasping voice call, 'Help me!'"

Joe watched Rachel absently rub away the goose bumps on her arms. At that instant he was convinced she'd forgotten he even existed. "What did you do?" he asked, despite the tingling he could feel at the back of his neck and along his arms.

"What I'm trained to do when someone's been hurt. I ran to find him."

"Did you?"

"Oh, yes. He was on the opposite side of the road, lying against one of the steel buttresses."

"Who was he?"

She closed her eyes. Just when Joe wondered if he had to repeat the question, she said in a lower pitch, "I didn't know. Not at first. Being relatively new in town, all I could tell was that I hadn't seen him at the clinic or anywhere else. I only knew his condition was critical, so I crouched down, intent on helping him any way I could. But the moment I reached for him," she added, her voice growing tense, "the moment my fingertips..." She shook her head and met his direct gaze. "He vanished."

Joe felt as though she'd turned a firehose on him. "He *what?*"

"I know it sounds incredible, but please hear me out." She pressed a hand flat to her chest. "Believe me, by the time I got back here, I had myself convinced the whole thing had been a figment of my imagination. But the next day I woke to find the weather the same. That was still all right, except that during the day more and more people started commenting about how unusual it was for this time of year and, naturally, it made it virtually impossible to put the incident behind me."

She paused, but Joe remained silent, determined not to help her make a fool out of him.

"Well, after closing the clinic I got to walk back here again. I was glad, hoping it would quiet my overactive imagination, as well as resolve my doubts once and for all."

"You're not suggesting it happened again?"

"No, not suggesting. It happened. Except that I was a little earlier this time. Not much, maybe a minute or so." She looked directly at him, but made him feel as though he was as transparent as refrigerator wrap. "It made a difference, at least in that he was somewhat more coherent. But also as before, when I tried to help him, he vanished."

Joe uttered a short, disgusted laugh. "I deserve this."

"Don't get angry."

"Angry? Lady, I should—"

"Listen to me!" She left the window and rounded the bed. "Yesterday I got a hunch. I thought, What would happen if I closed the clinic a few minutes earlier? Would he still be there? Would I arrive at a point where we could communicate more? My curiosity was relentless. I don't think I slept more than a half hour all night. By morning, when I saw the weather hadn't changed, I decided I was going to try it."

Joe thought that must have gone over real well with the hierarchy.

"It was a risk," she said, as though reading his mind. "One I'm paying for now. What I said to Jewel is only partly true. Sammy does think I'm suffering from fatigue. But the reason he's put me on mandatory leave is because I closed early and…and because I wouldn't tell him why."

What could he possibly say? That he was sorry? That nothing had changed and he still thought she was crazier than those two troublesome females downstairs?

"Was it worth it?" he found himself muttering.

"Frighteningly so." She moistened her lips, winced and touched the bruised one fleetingly. "Because my hunch was right. I reached him while he was still standing. Shot, like before, but standing. Once again he called out, but…this time when I approached him, he said my name as though he knew me. As though we were…as though we'd known each other for some time. Then," she added, bowing her head, "he said something that was even stranger."

Joe uttered a brief, harsh laugh. "So far everything you've said defies credibility."

"He begged me not to come back here," she continued, the urgency in her voice growing. "Not to meet someone. He said he was beginning to understand some of what was happening and that he didn't want me involved. And then…then he touched me. I'd been determined not to make contact with him, despite the obvious pain he was suffering, but I couldn't get out of reach fast enough. Just as his fingers brushed against my cheek, he disappeared again."

As though rising from a trance, she looked at him, her expression bruised-looking but direct. That, as much as anything else, edged Joe toward fury.

"What's supposed to happen now? Do you expect me to tell you that I believe you?" he ground out. "Well, I don't."

"No, of course not."

"Then why waste my time?"

"Because that poor soul on the bridge had suffered a gunshot wound to the stomach," she cried, her hands clenching into fists. "Oh, God, do I have to spell it out for you? When I asked him his name, he told me he was you! *Joe Becket.*"

CHAPTER THIRTEEN

Twice now she'd managed to knock him off balance and twice he'd stood there and let her do it. With his hands placed on his hips, Joe counted nails in the hardwood floor. It seemed a lot safer than shaking the truth out of her.

"Maybe you think I've been smelling too many fumes from those diesel trucks racing up and down that road out there," he said at last, "but, lady, I've got news for you. I'm not far enough gone to buy into what you're selling."

"I'm not—"

"*Knock it off!*" he roared, needing an outlet for his temper and taking it out on the open closet door. He'd meant to slam it shut, but instead missed, slicing his palm against the edge. With a curse he was sure the good doctor had never heard in the refined halls of her privileged home, he grabbed his hand and bent at the waist.

"Now you've done it," she muttered, rushing to his side.

"Leave me alone."

"It's probably bleeding again."

Hell, it should be falling off, considering how it felt. The strobe lights hadn't stopped flashing in front of his eyes yet, but he felt a telling dampness beneath the gauze, confirming she was right.

"Come with me into the bathroom and I'll see how bad the damage is."

He thought his bitter, answering laugh delineated his slim hold of his control. "Don't you think you've done enough? No, of course not. You won't be satisfied until I'm dead, will you?"

"Need I remind you that you're the one who's been threatening me?"

"Keep it up and I promise I'll do more than threaten." Despite her stung expression, he held on to his ire. "You're either ringy as hell or one helluva lousy actress. Whichever, get this—I don't need or want a Florence Nightingale in my life. Insist on sticking your nose where it doesn't belong, and you're asking for major trouble. Understand?"

"I'm going to get my bag."

But before she could do more than unbolt the lock, he had her spun around and pressed flat against the enameled-white door. He held her there with his body to save his hand. "I'm the one who says where you're going and when," he said, his face so close to hers he could count the charcoal-brown lashes on her eyelids.

There'd been more than a few hard-core felons who had backed down from him when he'd been in this mood; Rachel Gentry merely met his glare with shaky but impressive determination. "Or else what?"

Her solemn defiance ate away at his resolve in the same way her sleek curves tempted needs and dreams long repressed. "You don't want to know," he countered, a simmering something compelling him to skim his hand over her cheek and down her throat. But the moment he saw the streak of blood he left on her shirt, it stunted his temper and ardor like a blunt hatchet. He recoiled, staring.

After noting the damage herself, she murmured,

"I'll go change. I can rinse this out after we see to your hand."

This time he didn't stop her, but he didn't give her any privacy, either. He followed, halting in the doorway of her room because, he reasoned, she might have a gun herself.

She went straight to her dresser, self-conscious—he saw that in the arrow-straight line of her back—but unbuttoning her blouse regardless. It gave him the strategic benefit of a dual view, thanks to the dresser's mirror. He wasn't, however, willing to admit that he'd been fantasizing about finding himself in a moment like this for a long while.

She pulled open the top drawer and, reaching inside, lifted her gaze to his in the mirror. The glass was old, the kind that darkened with time and tended to create a surreal, shadowy reflection rather than a real one. It made the moment all the more dangerous—and erotic. How far would she go either way? he wondered, mesmerized.

Ever so slowly, purposefully, Rachel brought out a violet-blue tank top and placed it on the dresser. No fast moves. He admired how quickly she understood the rules. After carefully sliding shut the drawer, she eased the blouse off her shoulders, leaving her in only a woman's white T-shirt.

Maybe she understood them too well, he thought, his mouth going dry. When she pulled the shirt from the waistband of her jeans in an unhurried glide, he had his answer.

Desire slithered through him. It felt like a snake in writhing torment.

Still, he watched.

Her arms crossed, she lifted the top, exposing

smooth skin and a shape that had as many angles as
it did subtle curves. It gave her a focused sensuality
that spoke to him far too fluently.

Still he absorbed.

Exposed to the heavy, damp air and his gaze, her
nipples beaded. When she finally drew the shirt off
in one fluid sweep, he saw they were also toffee
brown and small, and his desire became as ruthless
as a dull knife. It dug deep into his gut...deeper, until
he sought relief by imagining himself closing the distance between them, cupping her from behind, caressing the tight buds, and learning how long it took
to make her come apart while they both watched.

Still he stayed rooted in place.

By the time she slipped the tank top over her head,
he was as taut as blistered skin. But he endured the
bittersweet eternity it took her to finish tucking the
hem neatly into her jeans before drawling, "Not the
shy type, are you?" although his throat felt fresh from
a dip in a blasting furnace.

"You're the one calling the shots."

Rachel wondered if he would feel the heat of her
embarrassment as she passed him and stepped into
the hall. One thing was for certain—she didn't dare
analyze what had compelled her to behave so outra-
geously. Not that she'd ever thought of herself as a
prude. No female raised in a male-dominated family,
who'd gone into a male-dominated profession, could
walk away with any puritan attitudes intact. But she
shouldn't have been so blatant, so intentionally pro-
voking, just because he'd made her angry and had
hurt her feelings.

Face it. Realizing he has to be Joe is making you lose it.

It was true. Subjected to the juxtapositioning of realities, she felt trapped in a psychological web. When she looked into this Joe's eyes, no matter how angry he seemed to get at her, she kept having flashes of the other Joe and how he gazed at her with torment and yearning. It left her confused and too vulnerable.

Rachel entered the bathroom and set her bag on the tub. "What's going to happen now?" she asked, turning to deal with the man's dislike as well as his wound.

"I haven't decided yet."

After loosening the adhesive strips, she began unwrapping the gauze. "You can't keep me hostage up here."

"Can't I? You said yourself that you're not expected at the clinic."

"What about your own job?"

"I got away to check on what you were up to. Mudcat's not going to doubt me if I tell him that my doctor insists I need some time off for this to heal," he said, nodding at his injury.

"All right, but then there's Jewel. She's suspicious of you. What if she goes to the police?"

"Something tells me that she doesn't like dealing with them any more than they must like dealing with her. In any case, you'd better pray she doesn't do anything foolish."

For a moment Rachel gauged his threat, but finally sighed and tossed the soiled gauze into the trash. "I'm not going to fight you."

"Smart decision."

"But I have one condition."

"*I* make the conditions."

"Tell me why you came here."

"Why did *you?*"

Confused, she shook her head. "You know why. I have a contract committing me to the clinic."

"Maybe that's your cover. What's your connection to Gideon Garth?"

Rachel thought she'd heard wrong. "The state senator?"

"Soon to be U.S. senator if he has anything to say about it. Are you going to tell me that as the daughter of one of Washington's most powerful lobbyists you've never made his acquaintance?"

"That's exactly what I'm saying. I've always made a point to avoid my father's business connections."

"What if I told you that I saw you talking to Garth's right-hand man this morning?"

She gave up trying to concentrate on the task at hand and stared at him. What in the world...? *Oh.*

Joe Becket smiled without humor. "What's the matter, giving up? You don't want to try to convince me that you don't know Wade Maddox either?"

"Actually, I do know him. Not well, but more than I'd care to." The uneasiness she'd felt while in Maddox's company returned anew, and she didn't bother trying to hide her revulsion. "He brought someone into the clinic one night. The man's injuries looked suspicious, but when I questioned him about it, he dismissed them as a joke."

"And your meeting with him on the bridge?"

So, he'd been watching then, too. "That was a coincidence."

"What did he say to you?"

"Nothing. He was just...talking."

Joe's mouth flattened into a hard, cruel line. "If you expect me to try to trust you at all, you'd better start again."

"He wanted us to go out, okay?"

"And what was your answer?" Joe snapped back.

"What do you think it was?" Exasperated with the man, she secured the new bandage a little more tightly than she'd intended.

Joe swore and jerked free of her grasp. "Watch it."

"No, you watch it. Maybe I'm beginning to understand your need to be cautious about people, but I resent being linked to that—" she couldn't find a word that adequately described Wade Maddox "—person."

"I suppose you *are* more Garth's type."

"Detective..." she ground out.

Before she could finish, he had one arm snaked around her waist; he jerked her close and clamped his good hand to her mouth so tightly she could barely breathe. "Don't call me that, damn it! Especially, not by an open door right above a frigging stairwell."

The speed and violence with which he'd moved once again exposed her to a ruthless side of him that she'd hoped was for intimidation only. But she was beginning to suspect she might be wrong. Knowing there was no way he could miss the subtle trembling of her body, she averted her gaze in defeat.

Slowly, he removed the hand over her mouth. Their bodies, however, remained intimately locked together as an unignorable threat.

"My God," she whispered, as a terrible revelation swept over her. "Please don't tell me this trouble you're in is because you did something wrong?" Although she hadn't known him long enough to feel

such things, she knew with a certainty that was as
bitter as a cold winter morning that she would be
devastated to hear it.

"Oh, that's good. That's very good," Joe drawled.
"Play innocent until you learn where the tape is. I've
got to hand it to Garth, he really hit gold by hiring
you for this job."

The man was beginning to sound like a broken record, and she was getting heartily sick of it. "I told
you, I'm not... What tape? Is this about blackmail?"

"No. Justice. I'm going to bring the SOB to his
knees for what he did to a friend of mine. And for
what he's planning to do to his constituents and this
country. That is, if I can stay alive long enough. But
believe me, if I don't, it won't be because I let you
put a knife or a bullet in my belly."

Rachel decided it would be a waste of breath to
declare her innocence again. On the contrary, she
wanted, needed more information. "Why don't you
tell me what he's done?" she suggested instead.

Joe uttered a harsh laugh. "You really are relentless."

"Because like it or not I'm involved!" she snapped
back at him, summoning what was left of her courage.
"And believe me, I'd prefer not to be. But Monday
night put me in the wrong place at the wrong time.
Ever since, my life has been turned upside down. I'm
tired, I'm a nervous wreck and I'm up to my rear end
in trouble with my boss. The way I look at it, you
owe me an explanation!"

He remained still and quiet, his gaze boring into
hers as though he willed to strip away her veneer and
see the truth for himself. Then he blurted out, with

no inflection whatever, "Garth had the woman I was seeing murdered."

Debilitated by the man's relentless inspection, and expecting the worst, the word *murdered* made Rachel's legs all but buckle beneath her. She sought and found the support of the cooler tiles behind her. "I'm sorry. I had no idea." But she needed to know now. "Tell me why—please."

At first he looked as though he would refuse, as though he couldn't believe he'd said as much as he had. But after a moment he awkwardly began. "Her name was Terri. Terri McCall. She was a remote-camera operator for one of the Houston TV stations."

"You're from Texas?" She bit her lip when he scowled at her interruption.

"We were at her place one afternoon when she happened to look out the window and spot Garth going to the apartment across from hers with a woman Terri recognized. Someone who was known to have a strong affiliation to a rapidly growing white supremacy group."

Rachel didn't know what to say. Everything she did and everything she focused on was directed to helping people, not on what caused strife or bloodshed. In the end she said nothing.

"Terri grabbed for her personal camcorder and called me to the window at the same time," Joe continued, clearly caught up in his own memories and pain. A white tension line appeared around his mouth. "She got some great footage. Enough to implicate Garth as being more than casually acquainted with the group. What neither of us realized until too late was that we were both spotted. Before the night was

PLAY SILHOUETTE'S

LUCKY HEARTS
GAME

AND YOU GET

FREE BOOKS!
A FREE GIFT!
YOURS TO KEEP!

TURN THE PAGE AND DEAL YOURSELF IN...

Play **LUCKY HEARTS** for this...

exciting FREE gift!
This surprise mystery gift
could be yours free

when you play **LUCKY HEARTS!**
...then continue your lucky streak
with a sweetheart of a deal!

1. Play Lucky Hearts as instructed on the opposite page.

2. Send back this card and you'll receive 2 brand-new Silhouette Intimate Moments® novels. These books have a cover price of $4.50 each in the U.S. and $5.25 each in Canada, but they are yours to keep absolutely free.

3. There's no catch! You're under no obligation to buy anything. We charge nothing—ZERO—for your first shipment. And you don't have to make any minimum number of purchases—not even one!

4. The fact is thousands of readers enjoy receiving their books by mail from the Silhouette Reader Service™. They enjoy the convenience of home delivery...they like getting the best new novels at discount prices, BEFORE they're available in stores...and they love their *Heart to Heart* subscriber newsletter featuring author news, horoscopes, recipes, book reviews and much more!

5. We hope that after receiving your free books you'll want to remain a subscriber. But the choice is yours—to continue or cancel, any time at all! So why not take us up on our invitation, with no risk of any kind. You'll be glad you did!

Visit us online at

www.eHarlequin.com

The Silhouette Reader Service™—Here's how it works:

Accepting your 2 free books and gift places you under no obligation to buy anything. You may keep the books and gift and return the shipping statement marked "cancel." If you do not cancel, about a month later we'll send you 6 additional novels and bill you just $3.80 each in the U.S., or $4.21 each in Canada, plus 25¢ shipping & handling per book and applicable taxes if any.* That's the complete price and — compared to cover prices of $4.50 each in the U.S. and $5.25 each in Canada — it's quite a bargain! You may cancel at any time, but if you choose to continue, every month we'll send you 6 more books, which you may either purchase at the discount price or return to us and cancel your subscription.

*Terms and prices subject to change without notice. Sales tax applicable in N.Y. Canadian residents will be charged applicable provincial taxes and GST.

If offer card is missing write to: Silhouette Reader Service, 3010 Walden Ave., P.O. Box 1867, Buffalo, NY 14240-1867

BUSINESS REPLY MAIL
FIRST-CLASS MAIL   PERMIT NO. 717   BUFFALO, NY

POSTAGE WILL BE PAID BY ADDRESSEE

SILHOUETTE READER SERVICE
3010 WALDEN AVE
PO BOX 1867
BUFFALO NY 14240-9952

NO POSTAGE
NECESSARY
IF MAILED
IN THE
UNITED STATES

over, Garth had Terri...silenced. But not before she managed to get the tape to me."

"Is that the tape you think I wanted?" Rachel asked. When he didn't reply, she drew her own conclusions. "Why haven't you turned it in to your superiors?"

"Because Garth threatened my partner and his family," Joe shot back, his expression a mask of fury and pain. "Oliver's black. Do you understand how ugly it could get? He's been married barely a year and a half, and his baby girl isn't four months old. I couldn't subject him to that kind of danger, so I decided to try disappearing to buy time."

"Of all the places you could have gone, why here?" Rachel had been in Nooton long enough to have learned it was part of Gideon Garth's home parish. She'd even heard some sardonic comments that he owned most of it.

"I thought I'd be safest where he felt the most secure."

"Then what are you waiting for?" As soon as she said the words, she knew. "His declaration to run for the U.S. Senate," she breathed.

Joe inclined his head, his look unwavering. "And nothing's going to stop me."

Rachel tried to take in this new revelation. She felt sorry for his friend. His lover, she amended, feeling a helpless, painful twist inside at the thought of him with another woman. But she also felt a new surge of fear. For him. Joe Becket. Either of them. *Both* of them.

"Dear heaven, that's got to be what I've been seeing on the bridge night after night," she murmured, mostly to herself. "You're going to get yourself killed because of that tape."

Joe uttered a sound of exasperation or maybe even disgust. "For crying out loud, what's it going to take for you to stop that nonsense?"

She gave herself a mental shake and offered an apologetic smile. "I agree it's bizarre. But if you'll give yourself a chance to think about it, you'll see it makes as much sense as anything else. I suppose what we should do now is find out when you're supposed to get shot...and then we can focus on how to stop it."

"Do you hear what you're saying?" Joe said, making no pretense of hiding his scorn.

Rachel nodded, rubbing her arms because she suddenly felt cold again. "Yes. But I feel he's the only one who can give us any answers."

"Wait a minute," Joe said warily. "Who can?"

As though she'd been racing down a road only to find herself at a dead end, Rachel realized that not only was Joe totally confused about what she'd been telling him, he had no intention of opening his mind to any possibilities, either.

CHAPTER FOURTEEN

"**Y**ou," Rachel told him gently. "Or specifically the *you* on the bridge. I'm going back there tonight and see if I can learn more."

"I must've been nuts to think you would play straight with me."

His anger was understandable, if disappointing. Rachel had to rely on her greater, although modest, knowledge of the situation in order not to let it defeat her. Finished with his hand, she reached for and began rinsing out her stained shirt. "I know it's hard for you to—"

"Not hard," he ground out. "Impossible."

"Yes." How well she understood; up until Monday she thought she had a cool, logical mind herself. "I'm still finding myself looking back to my chemistry and psychiatry classes for something that might explain this. And on Tuesday, when no one was looking, I actually ran some tests on myself to make sure I hadn't developed something that was making me hallucinate."

So she most definitely understood how this mystery was thrusting Joe in unfamiliar, unwelcome territory. Unlike her, he hadn't had the added benefit or influence of *seeing* the apparition and was no doubt feeling at a loss as to how to deal with this. It was too abstract. Too uncontrollable.

Which was why, when she finally hung the shirt over the shower rod to dry, she was neither surprised, nor did she resist as he took hold of her wrist and pulled her down the hall. She simply snatched up her bag and let him.

Once they were back in his room, Joe quickly released her. Not missing the undercurrents of that, Rachel placed her bag on the floor by the bureau and gave him the space he seemed to need by setting herself on the far side of the room against the wall by the window. Joe remained posted by the door. At least this time he didn't close and lock it, she thought. Every extra bit of air helped keep her from feeling suffocated.

"You don't have to stand guard," she told him, unable to keep totally silent about the way things looked. "I'm willing to stay…at least until around 1:00 a.m."

"You're not going anywhere then either."

"I have to. I told you, it's our only chance to learn more."

She was pushing her luck; he let her know it by shooting her a hard look from under his dark eyebrows. But she also saw him finger the package of cigarettes in his pocket. It gave her the courage to try another approach.

"There's another alternative to arguing," she murmured, careful to keep her voice low and empathetic. "You can come with me."

He laughed. It wasn't a reassuring sound. "Just what I want, an escort to an ambush."

"What's it going to take to convince you that I am *not* involved with those people?" she cried, leaning toward him.

"Someone else confirming your story, for one thing."

"You don't ask for much."

"Uh-huh. Isn't it slightly strange that no one else has seen anything out of the ordinary going on up there, except you?"

"Yes, it's bothered me. And I've come to the conclusion that if someone has, they're afraid to say anything for fear of being ridiculed. Then again, the phenomenon seems to happen strictly at night. In the three days I've been seeing you—it," she amended, when he again glowered at her, "I've only seen two trucks crossing the bridge. Considering the speed they were going, and add to it the poor visibility, I have to face the probability that I'm the sole witness."

"How convenient."

Rachel sighed and combed her hands through her hair. "So what do we do now?" she asked, as silence stretched between them. "Just stand here and stare at each other?"

"Have a seat, if you want."

She glanced at the bed. The thought of curling up and shutting her eyes and mind for a few hours was more than a little appealing, but she couldn't. Not on his bed—it reminded her too much of the way they'd been lying there before. To keep her imagination in check, she went to the chair by the bureau and removed several days' worth of newspapers piled there, dumping them on the floor.

Once she sat down and stretched her legs before her, Joe slid to the floor, his back braced against the doorjamb, his view of her unimpeded. Rachel considered his quiet scrutiny and knew she needed some other questions answered. "Do you watch me a lot?"

"I've been keeping an eye on everyone."

"That must cut into your rest a great deal."

"I'm not going to fall asleep, if that's what you're waiting for."

His sarcasm did nothing to offset the chemistry churning between them; on the contrary, it amplified it. Rachel decided to use the chemistry, because without some powerful impetus, she and Joe had little hope of achieving any real communication.

"I'm not," she said. "I just feel sorry for you, that's all."

"Well, don't."

She waited a few seconds before asking, "Don't you want to know why?"

"Did you hear me ask?"

Ignoring the rebuke, she continued, "Up until this week I'd always assumed cops found the role of voyeur as natural, maybe even entertaining in a way, but I think it's been difficult for you. I mean, following my every move, but fighting not to get emotionally involved."

"Fishing for a compliment, Doctor?"

"No. I'm trying to tell you that I know you're being deliberately cruel as a result of your ambivalent feelings toward me."

"Ambivalent? And what makes you think they're that? No," he said, grimacing. "Let me guess. You're going to say 'hindsight'?"

Rachel nodded. "Whenever he's looked at me, talked to me...there's been an instant intimacy between us that's poignant as well as comfortable. I've come to the conclusion that it couldn't exist if you were going to continue chewing me up and spitting me out as you've been doing."

Joe leaned his head back against the doorjamb with a thump and shut his eyes. "What's it going to take to convince you that I don't want to hear any more of this?''

"Let me go see him tonight," Rachel said again, sitting forward eagerly in her chair. "And come with me. See for yourself what's happening."

"Nothing's happening except that you're driving me nuts."

She sprang from her chair and crossed to him. At the door she hunkered down so they were eye to eye. "You have to trust someone sooner or later."

"That's a matter of opinion."

"Yes, you do, Joe. What's more, I think I'm your last hope."

She could no more keep from touching him than she could block from her mind the memory of those heart-wrenching scenes on the bridge. The man might have huge walls built around his emotions to keep her out, but she had only to touch his wrist to feel his pulse leap and she knew—she *knew*—something strong and important bound them.

"Are you really?"

The feel of him grasping her hand and pressing something unpleasantly slick against her palm had her nearly falling on her backside. She wasn't aware he'd picked it up again until she found herself staring at Jewel's balled-up candle wax.

Joe watched Rachel throw it to the floor and rub her palm against her thigh. "Get rid of that thing," she said. "Please."

Instead he scooped it up and, fascinated by her wary and repulsed expression, began tossing the ball in the air, then catching it. "Why, Doctor, don't tell me you actually believe in the voodoo queen's mumbo jumbo?''

"It reminds me of that hideous thing she keeps in her pantry.''

Joe's interest sharpened. "You've seen what's in there?''

"Unfortunately. There's a shrine around something she calls 'Black Hawk.' She treats it like some... deity, but it has to be the most gruesome thing I've ever seen.''

"Well, well. So we agree on something, after all. I don't know whether to be reassured or concerned.''

Rachel frowned. "When did you see it? Jewel doesn't usually encourage visitors to her kitchen.'' Before he could reply, realization lit her face. "The beer.''

"I keep myself alert by trying to get in and out of there without her catching me. For all she knows, her spooks are ripping her off.''

"Don't you think she's figured it out when she finds the empty cans up here?'' she replied, her tone turning as droll as her expression.

"I usually carry them to the garage inside a rolled-up section of newspaper.'' Joe thought about his encounter with Jewel's icon and allowed a grim smile. "Spotting old Black Hawk, as you called him, must've taken ten years off my life.''

It was the fading of Rachel's own smile that made him realize what he'd said, and Joe's fleeting humor went out like a snuffed candle. The thought that he probably didn't have ten days, let alone ten years, made him wish he had an entire six pack right now, and that the few brief moments of camaraderie they'd just shared could have lasted longer. Life, he con-

cluded dismally, was getting damned stingy with its
gifts.

"You know, sometimes I've heard footsteps in the
hallway...or at least I've thought I have. I feel better
realizing they must have been you."

She sounded almost shy, a dangerously appealing
dimension to a woman he was learning could be mul-
tifaceted at will. God, he needed to get out of here
before he gave in and made a fool of himself with
her. But there was nowhere to go—at least, not yet.
A few days from now would be another story. Garth's
deadline to announce his candidacy was only days
away. He thought if he could survive just a few more
days...

Crushing the wax in his fist, he said, "I want to
believe you, but this is my life we're talking about
here...Rachel."

A myriad of emotions flooded her lovely eyes—
surprise, pleasure, hope...gratitude. And then she surprised him by placing her palms together and touching her clasped hands to her lips as though in prayer.

"I know," she whispered. "Believe me, I do
know."

Maybe. But where did that leave him? He knew
her to be correct on one point—he wasn't going to
get through this without someone else's help, even if
only to have that person running interference for him,
keeping the duchess and the voodoo queen off his
back, and the like.

He eyed the black ball. Was Rachel the one to do
that for him? Could his instincts be so off that he
could want her to the extreme that he became blind
to what lay beyond that desire? Up until this mess,
he'd always been such a sharp judge of people.

"Ask me any question you want," Rachel said, scrambling closer and onto her knees. "Make any condition you want. I'll swear on anything you want that I'll stay in here with you without complaining. You can even handcuff me to the bedpost, if you want."

"This is not a good time to tell me you're into kinky stuff, Doctor," Joe drawled, because bad humor was a helluva lot safer than telling her how the idea and her rapt expression appealed to him.

"Please, Joe. Come with me to the bridge tonight. Let me see if I can make contact one more time."

Maybe if she hadn't used his name, his first name, he might have found the will to resist. But she did, and it sounded so right coming from her lips that his masochistic mind replayed it again and again; all the while he saw her, them together, a tangle of limbs, a blending of shuddering breaths, until reality and fantasy became a red blur of need.

He exhaled in pain. "One condition."

"Anything."

He uttered another silent oath as his body reacted swiftly to her offer. "I don't want to hear another word about...about what you think we'll..."

"Do?"

"Exactly."

Rachel's glance dropped down to the ball he was caressing with his thumb. "All right. May I have that?"

"No. I'm going to go flush it down the commode. You got a problem with that?"

"Since I had a similar idea, none whatsoever. I'll wait here."

That reminded him of his gun, and the tape he'd

noticed she hadn't yet located. As much as he hoped she wouldn't use his absence to try to reach either, he would be a fool to assume anything. "On second thought—" he tossed the hunk of wax to her "—who am I to deny a lady?"

CHAPTER FIFTEEN

"Are you okay?"

Rachel's question had Joe drawing in a deep breath—to purge some of the tension strangling him as much as to replenish himself with the night's moist air. After checking the gun tucked in the waistband of his jeans, he replied, "Yeah, but I'd feel even better if we were away from the porch light."

Fog or no fog, it made them sitting ducks; so, allowing himself to barely touch Rachel's arm, he directed her up the dirt road to blend in with the elements. Except for a quick glance that told him she'd noticed his restraint, she obliged him. She moved with the sleek, smooth speed he couldn't help but admire. Having repressed his awareness of her for over twelve hours now, he told himself that at any moment he should be adjusting to the psychological torture. He was more than ready. But he felt as though he was carrying a lead weight in his belly. No doubt the sandwiches they'd eventually gotten from downstairs helped. But it had less to do with the fact that he disliked the bread the voodoo queen had used than his inability to ignore his feelings for Rachel.

She shivered and wrapped her arms around herself.

"What's up?" Joe asked, instantly alert and peering into the dense night. All his senses were keyed to sense trouble before it found them. When he didn't notice anything, he demanded, "What's wrong with you?"

"I can't believe you're asking me that considering what we're about to do."

"What you *say* we're about to do."

She stopped in her tracks and gaped at him. In a way he understood that, too. After agreeing to do this, he knew she'd gotten the impression he was beginning to believe her, and maybe he thought something had spooked her. But what he was really doing was trying to prove to himself that she wasn't a lie. From his point of view, those were two different things.

Pretending he'd missed her stare, he nodded toward the bridge. "C'mon. Let's get this over with."

His behavior left Rachel more subdued than ever. It was for her own good, he told himself, knowing that was untrue. The fact was, any display of excitement made her all the more captivating to him, an added torment he didn't need. As far as he was concerned, the quieter he could get her, the safer for him.

As they approached the bridge, his unease broadened to include their surroundings. A car rambled by, and then a noisy pickup. He recognized both vehicles, the first belonging to some crusty old buzzard who owned a junkyard at the northern edge of town, and had a complaint about everything and everyone in the world. The pickup's driver was a drinking buddy of Mudcat's whose aggressiveness grew with each six-pack of beer he consumed.

But neither of them was what bothered him. It was something physically oppressive, and by the time they stepped up onto the pavement, it took Joe a moment to realize he wasn't winded, he couldn't go any farther because something was blocking his way.

"What the hell…?"

Already up on the sidewalk, Rachel swung back to

him. "What's the matter? Don't lag now, we're almost there."

"I can't."

"But, Joe, you said—"

"I said I *can't*," he snapped, his unease getting the best of him. "I didn't say I didn't want to."

She shook her head. "I don't understand."

"That makes two of us." Instead of meeting her somber scrutiny, he searched for visual confirmation that an obstruction was indeed blocking his way. "Somehow, something is stopping me from getting up on the damned bridge, Doc."

It was the oddest thing he'd ever experienced, but he was finally forced to meet her concerned look and offer a helpless shrug. He didn't know what to do.

She reached out to him and took hold of his good hand. "Try with me. You can do it."

Nothing interfered with her movements. He found that as unnerving as what was happening to him. He tried to follow her, but as soon as he was parallel to the first inch of steel girder, he came flush with an invisible but unbreakable barrier.

"Good Lord," she whispered, standing on the opposite side.

Joe decided it gave new meaning to the expression "so close, yet so far." "Looks as though you'll have to go on ahead," he told her.

"Not without you. You need to be there more than me."

"Apparently not. It seems this is as close as I'm allowed to get." What did get through to him was that in a way he'd just received his proof something unusual was indeed happening here. When he told her that, he had to smile at her startled look. "Didn't think of that yet, did you? Go on now," he added. "Do whatever you feel you need to do."

"I don't know what to say."

"Just be careful."

Rachel felt torn. In a way that was nothing new; she'd been feeling split since she'd realized she'd been dividing her attention, maybe even her loyalties, between two men who were ultimately the same person. But this feeling had less to do with that than with fear.

Why was Joe being denied access? The reason could make all the difference. Was it so that he wouldn't interfere with what was happening, or was it because he mustn't change things?

Oh, great, Gentry, next you'll be spouting that karma and destiny stuff.

It was too confusing. She did, however, take strength in the change she sensed in him. Maybe he wasn't completely convinced she wasn't working for Senator Garth's people, but there were large cracks in his theory. She saw it in his eyes and she'd heard it when he'd told her to be careful.

Nodding, she backed away from him, two steps...three. The more distance she put between them, the more his expression began to resemble the Joe she was about to search for—yearning, possessive. Almost tempted to run back to him to say God only knew what, she spun around and broke into a sprint toward the center of the bridge.

The fog enveloped her in its myopic reality. Checking her watch, she barely made out that she had about six minutes' leeway from her previous visits. What effect would that have on things? Would she see anything?

"Joe?" she called softly as she approached the spot where they'd been meeting.

There was no sign of him. Not even the bullfrogs' or tree frogs' night music could break through the laboring cloud engulfing her...and yet she felt a presence.

"Joe?"

She heard footsteps behind her. Behind her? How could that—She whirled around and saw him walking toward her.

Yes, it was him. But which one? she wondered, her heart doing an erratic skip.

And then she knew.

The fog kept his secret until he'd almost reached her. It was then she suddenly noticed a vagueness about him, a translucent quality that made him almost one with the mist.

"What's wrong?" she asked, anxiety wrenching a pain in her chest. "What's happening?"

"I don't know."

"I can barely see you."

"I'm getting weaker."

At least the wound wasn't present. Rachel took hope from that. "Is that good or bad news for you?" she asked, her hands clenched.

"There's only what is and what will be." Although his tone was enigmatic, his gaze was every bit as intent and mesmerizing as before. Then he swung away, uttering a tortured sound that seemed torn from him. "Why won't the craving weaken, too?"

It was as hard to hear him as to see him, and Rachel followed as close as she dared. "I don't understand."

"I can't stop thinking about you," he ground out as though each word brought him pain. "How it was between us. I can't let the memories go, Rachel."

His passion and anguish broke her heart. "What can I do? You have to help me to help you."

"If you wanted to help, you should have listened. Why did you meet him?"

His rebuke stung. "You know it was inevitable. And why do you keep talking about him as though he was a stranger? He's you!"

"Oh, Rachel, don't you get it? He's not me. I'm *him*. The thing he'll become because he won't be able to deny you."

Horrified, Rachel tried to take that in, but found it too much. "You can't mean…this is *my* fault?"

"It's no one's fault. You're only following your own…" He tried to speak, but Rachel realized he could no more explain than the other Joe could get on this bridge. "The old woman understands—" he began, and stopped suddenly, his attention drawn behind him. "They're coming. It's time to go."

"No, please. Wait," Rachel cried. "What old woman? Joe? How can I help you if you…"

She heard it, too. The sound of an approaching vehicle coming from where she'd left Joe. But as she started worrying about him and whether he'd been spotted, she was blinded by headlights and lost sight of his ghost.

Covering her eyes, she determined the vehicle was low, a car, not a truck. About to leap out of its way, it vanished.

"Joe!" she screamed into the swirling gray mist. The distant, but profound echo of a shot made her recoil as though it had struck her. "Joe…? *Joe!*"

* * *

He heard her scream from the end of the bridge, and it went through him like a bullet. With his heart in his throat, he grabbed his gun and broke into a sprint. He didn't realize until he was a dozen yards across the bridge that he hadn't hit the invisible wall this time.

Please, he prayed, *please*.

They almost collided in the middle of the road. He grabbed her to keep from knocking her to the ground, while she wrapped her arms around him and clutched tightly.

"Where are they?" he rasped, ready to drag her out of the line of fire.

"It's all right. They're gone."

"Are you sure?" He stroked her hair and held her close, absorbing her shaking body while he searched the fog. For death. He could feel it. Smell it.

"Joe," she whispered.

"I'm fine. C'mon, honey. Tell me who shot."

Her eyes went wide. "You heard?"

"It sounded kind of muffled, but yeah, I heard. I thought—God, I don't want to think about what went through my mind, I just knew I had to get to you."

It finally registered that he was on the bridge. He saw it reflected in her eyes, and he lifted his eyebrows in lieu of a shrug. "Don't ask me, I can't explain it." Then he grew sober again and scanned the area. "We've got to get away from here."

"Out of the street, maybe, but we're safe."

There was something about her voice, a numbness he didn't like. "What's wrong?"

"It's my fault. My fault."

Joe saw she was emotionally, psychologically wiped out. With a last glance around that made him decide there was no danger, he shifted his hold of Rachel and began leading her back toward the boardinghouse. "It'll be okay," he assured her.

He didn't try speaking again. He decided getting her away from there seemed the biggest priority.

Upon reaching the house, he tried his best to lock up as quietly as he could, but when he began to lead Rachel to the stairs, he was disconcerted to see someone step out of the shadows and approach them.

He began to reach for his gun...and recognized Jewel.

"She's got powerful trouble in the heart," she said, pausing at the balustrade and gazing up at a zombilike Rachel. "She needs time. Rest. You make sure she gets both, Mr. Police-*man*. Then you tell her to come see me."

Joe froze. She *knew*? "The last thing she needs is to get mixed up with a nickel-and-dime witch doctor," he threw back, figuring he had nothing to lose.

"Brave words for a dead man," Jewel sneered back.

That won an anguished gasp from Rachel. "Jewel!" she cried, reaching out as though to stop the word from reverberating in the darkness.

CHAPTER SIXTEEN

Joe wasted no time in getting Rachel upstairs and away from their viper-tongued housekeeper. He didn't want her defending him, not after what she'd been through. It bothered him enough that she looked drained and ready to collapse.

But she soon reminded him that it was a mistake to underestimate her. By the time they reached their floor, she'd collected herself enough to need almost no support. What surprised him the most, however, was discovering that he found himself leading her directly to her room instead of his.

Rachel seemed surprised, too. She looked up at him with an expression that brought a unique tightness to his chest.

"I don't know," he admitted, trying to explain. "Maybe I'm thinking you've earned it."

She leaned back against the door, and rocked her head back and forth. "No. That's the one thing I'm certain is not true. I should never have forced my way into your business. He made that clear tonight," she added, nodding briefly toward the bridge.

Joe had to ask. "Can you talk about it now?"

At first he thought she might not answer; then she replied, "He's getting weaker. I think...he'll be gone soon."

It felt strange to hear what she thought was him be referred to as though he was another entity entirely. Is that how she saw the apparition? She must for it—

for *him*—to have affected her so profoundly. Joe couldn't help feeling oddly resentful, jealous.

"What else?" he asked, unable to keep his voice as casual as he would have preferred. She heard the tension, or maybe the stiffness; he knew it by her suddenly surprised, guilty glance.

"I think I'm afraid to tell you."

"Rachel—" he took a calming breath "—whatever that force was or wasn't that kept me from joining you up there, it did make me accept that something unique was going on. I *want* to understand, if you'll give me the chance."

"I can see that. But you don't know how hard it's going to be to explain. You see, I think…it seems that what's going to happen will be my fault."

Was this part of an intricate plan to gain his compassion as well as his trust? He didn't want the doubts to resurface; nevertheless, they did, and he had to struggle to keep them contained. "Why do you say that?"

"Because I didn't listen to him. He'd warned me not to meet you and I did, anyway."

"How could you know?"

"Yes, that's what I thought. But it's not only that."

"Then tell me. Rachel, look at me and tell me."

She'd lowered her gaze to his chest. At his command, she lifted her eyes and let him see her own awareness of him. "He said you won't be able to deny me."

Those were words he understood, and their truth bound him with a heavy anchor chain and dragged him down, down, down. Within seconds, he felt as though his lungs would explode. This was what he'd been afraid of: that what was so powerful and real between them would grow, overwhelm, and demand its due.

"It won't happen," he told her.

"No, it mustn't," she agreed.

What didn't help was watching her eyes soften even more, with apology, compassion...yearning. Again he felt the strain of denying himself what he craved the most.

"We're not going to do this," he said gruffly, although he took a step closer to her.

"Because it's wrong," she said sadly.

"It wouldn't be wrong!" he ground out, stopping before her.

"It wouldn't?" She moistened her lips. "What would it be?"

Somehow his good hand shifted to her hair, her cheek. He knew he had to resist, and yet he wanted her. Dear heaven, he wanted her. "Dangerous," he rasped.

Nothing had ever been this hard. His mouth was mere inches away from relearning the lush, moist pleasure of hers. Their bodies were close enough to ignite from each other's heat. When her unsteady sigh caressed his chin and lower lip, he steeled himself against the pain of wanting to feel it, her, over every inch of him.

"Too dangerous," she agreed, averting her gaze.

"Try to get some rest." He reached around her, opened her door, which they'd left closed but not locked. "We both need some time and space. We'll talk about what happened in the morning."

"I won't be able to sleep."

He knew that. He wouldn't, either. He'd be busy

torturing himself with what could have been if life—
fate—had been different; not wanting to face the
knowledge that if things had gone differently, they
would never have met. "You have to try. It'll be
dawn soon."

For a moment he thought she would challenge him,
do something impulsive and insane like press her
mouth to his and push this beyond the point of con-
tainment. To his relief, after another few excruciating
seconds, she nodded her acceptance and wordlessly
retreated into the dark room.

"We will need to talk in the morning," he reminded her, backing away.

"Yes. Whatever you want."

"Don't I wish," he muttered, turning to his own
room.

"I wish." His last words to her echoed in her mind
and, despite her exhaustion, refused to let Rachel find
relief in sleep.

"I wish."

She did, too. An hour later, as she lay wide awake
in bed, she couldn't explain at what particular moment she'd known that, or how she could want him
so badly, while at the same time feeling a powerful
closeness to his ghost. And to her, they were two
separate entities, so different, like night and day, fire
and water, coldness and warmth; yet both of them had
broken through her defenses and were staking a claim
to her heart.

As though he felt the weight of her troubled
thoughts, Rachel heard Joe sigh and shift restlessly in
his own bed. A moment later he rose.

Every inch of her being listened. They'd both left

their doors open, an unspoken agreement she could have explained away with a half-dozen reasons, each of them legitimate. But when she heard the faint sound of his bare feet on the hardwood floors, her heart began to pound, and she knew the gesture had been done for this reason alone. They'd wanted to keep some form of connection, even if it was only the sound of his steps and the air shifting around his body.

What was he doing? Where was he going? The heat was unbearable; maybe he needed a drink of water. But when, instead, she felt him pause in her doorway, it was all she could do not to lift her lowered lids completely and acknowledge that she wasn't asleep, either.

Of course, she didn't. If he wanted her, she asked herself with brutal clarity, shouldn't he be the one to make the first move? The final decision?

Then she felt the hot caress of his eyes.

It was tormenting him. Had he changed his mind? Was he going to come to her bed and ask for what neither of them seemed strong enough to deny?

Unable to keep still any longer, Rachel sat up in bed. "What is it?"

He muttered something, an apology maybe, and turned away.

"Joe?" Rachel scissor-kicked herself off her bed and followed. "Joe."

He retreated to his room and shot back, "Don't come in here."

But Rachel didn't stop until she was inside. Didn't stop as he turned on her, although even in the dim light she could see his feral mood.

"I said don't," he half warned, half pleaded.

"I can't sleep, either. Maybe you'd like to try that talk now?"

Sometime since they'd parted he'd shed his T-shirt, and the sheen of sweat on his chest and arms caught the faint light in the room with every breath he took. "No. I don't want to talk."

"Then we'll sit together."

"Damn it, Rachel." He reached out and grasped her arm. Like a wild beast who'd realized it had hold of its prey, he quickly tried to perfect that control, shifting his grip on her neck, her shoulders, gentling only when he slid a hand back up to frame her face. "Rachel…"

"I know," she whispered.

His gaze worshipped, apologized and devoured. He tilted his head left, right and left again, as though turning on the axis of her mouth, as though torn between taking and resisting the temptation she represented. And his mouth was close, so close it hurt not to have it touching hers.

"It's killing me."

"Dangerous," she managed to get out, to remind him.

"So's breathing these days," he muttered bitterly. Finally, he stroked her lower lip with his thumbs and groaned, "I have to," before locking his mouth to hers.

She shivered as his passion poured free; she even answered his kiss, but left her hands limp at her sides. She knew she mustn't hold him. If she did, when it came time to end the moment, she might not be able to let go. It was enough to feel his gratitude and pleasure.

Then, clearly wanting more himself, he edged her

back against the wall and melded his body completely against hers.

Someone gasped.

Someone groaned.

Behind her closed lids, Rachel's universe contracted and expanded, colors exploded, all while Joe urged her to give him more, in a kiss that went on and on. She forgot to breathe, but didn't care. His greater weight threatened to crush her, and she barely noticed. All she wanted was to feel him pressing, rubbing, rocking against her, thrusting inside her, and to give him the oblivion they both direly needed.

Helpless to resist a moment longer, she wrapped her arms around him. It felt…unbelievable. Incited, his hands coursed a journey of exploration, and she stretched and arched into each blatant, intimate moment of discovery. But it wasn't enough.

Blissfully soon he sought more. He slid his hand to her thighs, reached under her nightshirt, and found her…naked.

"Ah—jeez," he rasped, palming her bottom. Quickly, desperately, he stooped and, burying his face against the side of her neck, he locked his hips more perfectly against hers.

He was aroused and she was burning, burning alive. To quench her thirst she sought his mouth again for a deep, plumbing kiss that soon matched the evocative dance he initiated with his hips. A low, yearning murmur rose from her throat; when he inched his uninjured hand around to her front and ventured to where she was alluringly hot and moist, it ended in a whimper.

Then he found that secret, vulnerable place, and Rachel cried out and instinctively struggled for freedom. It was too much. Too good. She couldn't possibly survive the sensations racking her body. But Joe wouldn't let her go.

"Don't fight me. Take it," he rasped, his skillful touch relentless. "Let me feel you wanting me. I need this, Rachel."

It came to her that she did, too. No one had ever cared to put her pleasure first. And to know her satisfaction mattered to Joe was as seductive, as erotic, as any of the sensitive things he was doing to her body.

She became a creature of reflex. Every muscle began to spasm, every nerve threatened to short-circuit in exquisite agony.

"Come on, Rachel...come on...come on..."

Suddenly, ecstasy claimed her and she felt ejected from her body, splintering and rocketing into space. Farther and higher she flew, clinging to Joe. Joe. "Joe."

"Why?" she whispered against his shoulder when she recovered the use of her voice again. "I wanted it to be with you."

"This time it will be," he replied, his voice thick with emotion. "But, the thing is...I wanted you to make me forget the night and reality. Only I wasn't about to ask for that without pleasing you first." He pressed a kiss to her forehead, her cheek, her lips. Then against them he whispered, "Rachel, help me. Help me escape my own mind."

From her point of view, it took an incredibly strong, *honest* man to admit his own needs and expose something as fragile as his vulnerability. When he added, "Help me make it to dawn," she could no more refuse him than she could have resisted his gifted touch.

Swallowing the emotions that blocked her throat, Rachel eased her hands between herself and Joe and released a few of the buttons on her shirt. Then she shrugged one shoulder, the other, and let the covering drop to her wrists and waist. Freeing her hands, she pushed the shirt the rest of the way to the floor.

CHAPTER SEVENTEEN

As he stared at Rachel, Joe discovered there was a certain type of torture he could develop a craving for. She was everything he'd dreamed, everything he wanted, everything, he concluded, as he braille-read her body with his hands. Slim, but with exquisite curves, she looked more feminine this way and ultimately too fragile for a man with his hunger. He was grateful she'd already proved her passion matched his.

He wanted to start arousing her all over again; then she reached for the zipper on his jeans, leaned close—so close he could feel her breath tease the hair on his chest—and his mind went blank to everything but the need to experience her hands exploring him. "Do it," he rasped.

Her lips were like warm silk against his taut, feverish skin. The faintest contact gave him a pleasure he thought he could happily die from—only to be launched onto a different plane of awareness and ecstasy when she spread another, prolonged kiss across his chest. At the same time, her knuckles brushed against his belly, making him suck in a quick breath through clenched teeth and wonder if he had the strength, let alone the patience, to let her set her own pace.

The moment he'd yielded to the need to check on her in her room, only to discover she was as wide awake as him, he'd known this was inevitable. Hav-

ing fantasized it again and again, he was already at
the end of his endurance, and his body ached as
though stretched on some medieval torture rack. Only
the fact that he'd been a bastard to Rachel and had
wanted to make up for some of that by putting himself
second to satisfying her had kept his desire in check.
But the problem was, she was so pretty, so sensual,
so damned tempting, she made him feel as though
this was his first time in every way; the memories of
being with other women vanished like ashes in the
wind.

But what undermined him the most was that she
was as bold and as honest about her desire for him
as he was toward her.

He closed his eyes, absorbing her touch. Then, unable to deny himself the visual delight of watching
her, reopened them. How could she look both wanton
and sweet at the same time? It's what had driven him
crazy during the days of his covert surveillance, and
the only lingering doubt he suffered now.

His rational mind told him that she was too good
to be true, that she could destroy him. His body told
him that if he didn't have her, and soon, it wouldn't
matter. Don't be a lie, he prayed, as her touch became
magic.

Slowly, she lowered his zipper and slid deft, sen-
suous fingers inside to explore him. As pain merged
with pleasure, a groan rose in his throat and he
scooped her into his arms. He carried her to the bed,
and followed after stripping off the rest of his things.
He'd endured enough, he told himself, covering her
with his body. Lingering doubts, the perplexing mystery of that damned bridge, his jealousy and greed to

have all of her for himself...none of it amounted to squat at this point. They would finish this now.

"Don't be a lie," he whispered, his voice so thick with emotion, the words were barely audible.

But Rachel caught it and her eyes cleared slightly. "What?"

"Nothing." He swooped down to lock his mouth to hers. It couldn't make any difference. No matter what, he thought, this was meant to be.

He abandoned himself to the dream. Their tongues tangled and tempted, their hands possessed and explored, until Joe raced them both closer to madness by thrusting himself between her thighs to seek the damp heat he'd ignited.

"Yes," Rachel breathed, shifting to wrap her legs around him.

Joe groaned. Unable to resist a moment longer, he slid deep inside her, felt her uncontainable shiver of ecstasy and let his body respond with its own reaction to their joining. She was sleek, hot, and it felt like heaven to be surrounded by her. But, not wanting to break the insulating effect silence offered, he told her by raining kisses over her face instead. And fought the temptation to yield quickly to release.

Not until they were both convulsing with need, he promised in the pulsating darkness. Not until he'd reached as deep inside her as he could go, he vowed, feeling her breath catch with his first powerful thrust. Not until the restless hands moving over his back and hips bit into him in frenzy, he swore, trailing his kisses to her throat and downward to her right breast.

And it became all that and more, shattering the silence with shallow breaths and gasps. The heat built, turning the room into a furnace that scorched them.

Joe's head—his entire body—pounded, ready, ready for an end to his waiting, and hers.

He raised himself on his arms, his muscles straining, droplets of sweat pouring off him and onto Rachel's exquisite form. Watching, seeing their joined bodies, made it all the more powerful, and at that moment it happened. With a groan of surrender and satisfaction, Joe yielded to Rachel's demanding pull, slid his hands deep into her hair and crushed his mouth to hers.

Reality returned despite Rachel wishing she could hold it at bay. She turned her head and looked out the side window, and remembered.

Now that the ravaging tide of passion was abating, she could think more clearly, and her thoughts were focusing on what Joe had said, but not, she began to comprehend, for her ears.

Don't be a lie.

She'd believed, with obvious foolishness, that they were past those doubts. After what he'd experienced on the bridge, he had to know that what was between them had nothing to do with his problem with Gideon Garth. It just illustrated again how he could be hard, relentless. And once again she had to face the contrasts between him and the Joe out there.

Yet, while they'd been making love, it had been everything. More than anything she could have dreamed. She sighed, as much as his weight allowed, only belatedly realizing it would attract his attention.

He raised himself on his elbows and followed her gaze. She could feel his body tense.

"Something wrong?"

"No." Rachel shifted, ready to assure him, but after meeting his unreadable gaze, she found it was easier said than done. "I'm okay," she murmured, looking outside again.

She didn't know what else to say to the man who'd just succeeded in bringing out a side of her she hadn't known existed, and a side of himself he could soon decide he hadn't wanted her to see. A man who was still very much alive inside her. Why did all of that make her feel guilty, as though she'd committed an act of betrayal?

"I must be heavy."

As he began to withdraw from her, Rachel was stunned by the power of the sensations he reignited within her. In a heartbeat, she knew that it would take very little to rouse her desire for him again. Sucking in a quick breath, she barely resisted reaching out to keep him close. But her reactions were enough to make him pause...then settle back onto his elbows.

Cautious, almost clumsy, fingers brushed a strand of hair off her damp forehead. "It may be a mistake to admit this, but it makes me jealous to think about where your thoughts are."

"I'm sorry. I'm trying not to do that."

Joe nodded, but his expression remained grim. "I know. But it's still hard. Even after what I experienced out there tonight. It goes against everything I've believed in for thirty-five years."

"You don't think I understand that? Do you think it's easy for me?"

"I don't know. You should see your expression when you look at that damned bridge, or now, when you talk about him even evasively. Do you even realize you're getting hung up on a ghost, Rachel?"

"His name is Joe Becket," she whispered entreatingly, as though through will alone she could make him see and accept what she needed to see in him. *Believed* was in him.

"He's not me, damn it!"

The quiet fury underlying his words, along with the memory of another, equally passionate declaration not long ago, had Rachel closing her eyes, because her instinct was to withdraw and there was nowhere to go. It did, however, seem to make a point with Joe, who sighed and once again stroked her hair.

"I'm the one who's sorry. For disappointing you. For having the inborn doubts that don't necessarily have anything to do with you. For not being able to keep my hands off you," he concluded, his tone going deep and gruff. "All I want is a few hours away from the insanity and the tension. Look, in the morning I promise to try to deal with whatever you want to talk about, but for the rest of the night...Rachel, there can only be you and me in this bed."

His expression was grim, almost as menacing as the first time she'd opened the bathroom door and come face-to-face with him. But there was also a haunting entreaty in his eyes that made her heart ache. It was underscored by the dismal wail of an unidentifiable animal somewhere outside. It so matched the earthy realness of the man towering above her that Rachel found it remarkably easy to reach up and stroke his beard-roughened cheek with the backs of her fingers before slipping her hand behind his head and coaxing him downward, downward to her breast.

"Then that's how it will be," she said as he parted his lips over her left nipple.

As currents of renewed desire stirred inside her, she let him lift her from the bed and reveled in his touch.

He was taking control again, and Rachel buried her fingers in his thick, dark hair and gave herself up to the heat building inside her.

This big, strong man, who could kill her as easily as make love to her, remained vulnerable at his core. Somehow she had to prove to him that she would never, ever betray that vulnerability.

Rachel parted her lips in welcome as Joe shifted to claim her mouth with his. She initiated the silent, provocative duel of tongue against tongue until she won a growl of approval and pleasure from him. She duplicated his restless exploration of her body by discovering the hard but responsive parts of his.

But when he slipped his fingers between them and deep into the dark curls where she burned, she could only hold her breath and hope she had the endurance to resist what he seemed to want to win from her again.

"That's not fair," she gasped, the instant he found the tiny bud of sensitivity.

"But it's good…and fascinating to watch. You, Rachel, coming apart for me. No one else but me."

So he was still staking a claim and making a point. Even after she'd agreed to share this bed and this moment, with him and him alone, he was making a not-so-subtle accusation and acknowledging his jealousy.

Rachel knew she shouldn't let him get away with it, but he chose that moment to roll his hips against her and convulse inside her, and she was lost.

Rachel reached up over her head, pressed her hands flat against the headboard, and yielded to the demands of both of their bodies.

CHAPTER EIGHTEEN

The red eyes appeared on the horizon of the blissful blue sea of Joe's tranquil dream. He didn't want them there; he wanted to continue floating on the raft with Rachel in his arms. But the eyes came closer and closer, growing from pin size to normal size, and larger. The bigger they got, the more hostility he sensed emanating from them, and the more hideous and deformed they looked.

Then they were directly before—no, over him. He tried to dodge their assault, rear back. It was a mistake.

Suddenly he was in a freefall. Rachel was ripped from his arms and he was falling…falling…

With a gasp, he opened his eyes and found Jewel standing over him. Her eyes weren't the hideous mutations in his dream, but they reflected enough hostility to let him know he never wanted to meet her in any dark alleys.

Right on the heels of shock came the awareness that it was well into morning, and that the gun he'd moved from under the box spring—once Rachel had gone to sleep—was still out of reach. If the voodoo queen had something deadly on the tray she was carrying, he didn't have a prayer of getting to it before she got him. And from the expression on her face, he knew she knew that.

Bad move not to have closed and locked the door, Becket.

True. But with the stifling heat, it had been slightly more bearable with both his and Rachel's doors open to create a modicum of a breeze. Had been. At the moment there seemed to be precious little oxygen in the room.

"Didn't waste much time taking advantage, did you?" the woman muttered with a scornful look, before shifting her gaze to Rachel, who was rousing in his arms.

"Jewel," Rachel murmured, her tone surprised and then wary. "What time is—Oh, Lord."

Joe had felt her start only seconds before she spoke. Not wanting to add to the tension and embarrassment he sensed in her body, he released her. She quickly tugged the sheet more securely over her breasts.

"You shouldn't be climbing all those stairs for us," Rachel added, when no one else seemed to be in a hurry to say anything.

"Did it for *you*," the housekeeper told her. "But now I can't say as I know why."

Rachel brushed her hair back from her face and struggled to sit up. "Don't say that. You don't understand."

Jewel lifted her turbaned head haughtily, the whites of her eyes growing wide as she glared. "Girl, the Widow Jack knows everything. But it's your funeral."

Joe felt Rachel tremble against him. "Don't say that, either."

"Bah!" With a toss of her head, Jewel shoved the tray onto the nightstand and stomped out of the room and down the hall. Her mutterings as she descended the stairs sounded as ominous as they were foreign.

Joe could sense Rachel's dismay and watched as

she glanced toward the window where it was easy to see the grayness remained unchanged once again. With a sound of despair, she drew up her legs and pressed her forehead against her knees.

He reached over and gently massaged her shoulder, much as he'd seen her do for herself. "Don't let her spook you," he said, fighting the need to drag her back into his arms.

"How can I help it? Every time I turn around, things seem to be going from bad to worse. I feel caught in the middle of some twilight zone or something."

He knew exactly what she meant, only he also knew she, at least, had an out. "It can end, you know. All you have to do is walk away. Leave Nooton."

That brought her head up, and she stared at him as though he'd suggested she rob the local bank. "How can you suggest such a thing after last night? You need me, Joe."

"I don't need you. I want you more than I want my next breath, but I don't need you."

He may as well have struck her; her expression turned that bewildered, that hurt. Her soft, insightful eyes scanned his face, and she slowly shook her head, laughed mirthlessly and looked away. "I knew you'd regret it in the morning. What I didn't expect is that you'd be so bitter about it."

"The hell you didn't."

It was a brutal thing to say, but he said it as much for her good as his own. He knew she was already too close to having control of his heart, and he needed to remind them both that last night's decisions were made with their eyes open; they'd known there would be a price to pay.

Nevertheless, when she uttered an unintelligible reply and tossed the sheet aside to scramble from bed, he reached out, caught her around the waist and dragged her back against him.

"Don't!" she cried.

"I'm sorry."

"No, you're not. You meant it. Nothing's changed at all. What's worse, you're tempted to continue testing me because you can't get past the suspicion that I may be setting you up."

Tired of the doubts, Joe swore under his breath and tried to ease his inner turmoil by stroking his beard-rough cheek against her hair. "Hasn't the reason for that occurred to you?"

Rachel went still, cautious. "Of course it has. You don't know how to trust. Me or anyone else for that matter."

"And why is that?"

"Because you've been a cop too long and you're hardened through and through."

"Sure I am," he replied, aware she was reacting to her wounded feelings, which allowed him to speak with more honesty than he might have. "But maybe I'm also a little scared. Maybe I'm a lot scared."

"Of what?" she asked, resentment lingering in her voice.

"You, for one thing. Some other things, but you most of all."

"Don't make me laugh. You're one of the most disciplined, awesome men I've ever met. I'm not in your league."

"That's what you think...and up until a few hours ago, you couldn't convince me that you were more than a beautiful, cold-blooded bitch. So much for us reading each other accurately."

Although she didn't answer right away, Joe felt the rigidity drain from her body. Slowly, he shifted his hold, and this time caressed her hair with his fingers, slow strokes that continued downward to trace the feminine line of her spine. At her helpless shiver, he grasped her right shoulder and she tilted her head to touch her cheek to his hand.

"Roddie used to say that judging people fairly and accurately was most people's downfall."

"Was he the one who died?" Joe didn't mean to resurrect painful memories, but they were *her* memories and he wanted to own a piece of them, too. Again, maybe not smart, he admitted, but necessary.

"Yes. He was an expert at being misjudged." As though needing something useful and immediate to do with her hands, Rachel reached for the pot of coffee and poured some of the steaming brew into the single matching cup and saucer Jewel had provided.

When she offered it to him, Joe shook his head, trying not to focus on the enticing picture she made and how tempting her uptilting breasts were. "She meant that for you. Besides, you look like you need it."

"We both do, but we'll share. Go ahead. It isn't poisoned," she insisted once she noticed he continued to hesitate.

"How would you know? That woman hates my guts."

"But as you said, she thought she was bringing this to me." She immediately turned back to the tray, moved it onto the bed and lifted the stainless serving cover from the platter. A huge omelet oozing with chopped ham, peppers and cheese, and accompanied by hash browns and toast smothered with Jewel's homemade jam, sent an aromatic temptation drifting up toward them. "Do you think we can keep from hurting each other long enough to do this justice?" she asked in a tired voice.

He gave up on thinking he could be hard-nosed and instead of giving her a verbal answer, snatched up a portion of toast and forced her to take a bite. "She's got incredible timing," he muttered. "I'll give her that."

They were silent for a few moments as they passed the coffee, then the fork so they could each get some food in them. At last, with the first pang of hunger appeased, Joe ventured, "You've never really allowed yourself to talk about what happened to him, have you?"

"Roddie, you mean? How did you know?"

"I may misjudge you when it comes to figuring out what I want from you, and what I think you want from me, but you can't hide from your dreams."

She pushed a piece of mushroom with her fork. "Did I talk in my sleep?"

"Not last night. But you have in the past, and I've heard you." Joe reached over and exchanged the fork for the coffee cup. "Why don't you tell me about him?"

Rachel delayed making any response by taking another longer drink of the coffee and afterward refilling the cup. She didn't want to talk about Roddie, not now when there were other problems, equally sad— perhaps soon to be equally tragic—to contend with.

Yet because he'd asked, she knew she couldn't shut him out.

"To understand Roddie, *why* he did what he did, you'd have to know what my father and older brother are like. Are you sure you want to hear all that?"

"You said it yourself—we're not strangers anymore. Doesn't intimacy demand its own price?"

She'd already begun paying hers; she felt it with every painful beat of her heart. "All right." She focused on the twisted sheet riding up at their feet and took comfort in how it exposed how close they lay together. "Kirk is my oldest brother and he remains very much my father's son—ambitious, political and ruthless. Once my father decided he wanted him to go to West Point, Kirk went. My father told him to become a career officer, and he did. Someday he'll be told to retire and enter politics, and Kirk will."

"You don't approve?"

"I don't believe in feeding into a system, any system, but especially a political one. As a lobbyist my father is always seeking another foothold in the metaphorical door, searching for someone else to use, establishing another link in the almighty networking chain. Don't be fooled, his choices for Kirk have never had anything to do with paternal pride, they have to do with his personal goal for power."

"Lord—you are angry."

"You wanted to hear. Listen. Roddie was several years younger than Kirk and different. Gentler, more sensitive, he wasn't meant to follow in Kirk's footsteps and he tried to tell my father he didn't want to be another 'mental gladiator,' as he called it. The truth is, he didn't know what he wanted to be, and my father wasn't interested in waiting for him to find out, let alone listening. I think Roddie's softness embarrassed him.''

''But you two were close?''

''Not in character or temperament. But we respected each other's ideals and dreams. We were also supportive of each other's right to determine our own future and to make our own mistakes. Unfortunately, I wasn't enough to buffer the battering ram of my father's anger or our mother's chiding. Barely two months after he got to West Point he was expelled. An upperclassman accused Roddie of making indecent overtures.'' She shrugged, still unsure what really happened.

''We'll never know the truth, but my father was furious. I'd never seen him so angry—not violently angry, but cold. Brutal. For all his shortcomings, Earl Harper Gentry *is* eloquent,'' she noted sardonically. ''He sliced Roddie to shreds and crushed what was left of his spirit into the ground. A few hours later Roddie shot himself.''

''And you found him,'' Joe finished for her.

So he remembered their previous conversation, as well. Rachel nodded and took another sip of coffee. ''His death changed me. From that moment on I was determined to live separate and away from the Earl Gentrys of the world.''

It was a full minute before Joe asked, ''What plans did your father have for you?''

''Oh, he thought I should study law at his alma mater. Exactly what the world needed, don't you think?'' Her laugh was bitter. ''But I wasn't going to be just another lawyer, oh, no. He saw an eventual bench seat and, ultimately, a supreme court position on my horizon. The man does not think small.'' Then she sighed, partly in relief and partly fatigued by the mere thought of all that wasted cunningness. "Imagine the power he would have had with one offspring running the country from the oval office or at least the senate, while the other helped legislate his dogma. His only regret was that my mother couldn't give him other children so he could cover more territory."

"Having a doctor in the family isn't too slouchy," Joe said, taking the cup from her hands and replacing it with the fork.

Rachel didn't protest, but put it down, her appetite gone. "What good was a doctor to him? No, he fought me. Hard. But I wouldn't give up any more than I could forgive him for what he'd done to my brother. In the end I saved him the trouble of having to disown me by moving out on my own. That's why I had to take out those loans I told you about."

"And the rest, as they say, is history?"

"More or less."

"You know your father's not the only willful person in your family," Joe drawled.

"I never said drive and focus were bad. It's where you direct it that matters."

"Like at me, for instance?" His voice was smooth, as seductive as the backs of the fingers he stroked down her left breast and across her nipple.

Rachel felt her focus slip and couldn't keep from shivering as needles of pleasure danced through her body. However, she managed to hold his unreadable gaze. "Yes. But only for the best reasons. Which brings us back to square one, doesn't it?"

"Looks that way. Getting dizzy yet?"

For the most part he'd been respectfully reticent throughout her explanation, but now Rachel wondered if that had been shrewdness instead? What *was* going on in his mind? He gave so little away. "Joe, I stay dizzy around you, and I think you like it that way. But there's one thing I'm clearheaded about and that is that time's running out for you."

He attempted a sardonic smile, but it didn't quite form...and, like hers, his appetite suddenly seemed to disappear. "I've got to go with my gut hunches, Rachel. And my gut hunch says I'd better see my plans through to the end or else I won't get another chance. I can't sit back and let Garth get elected."

"What does that do to us?"

He bowed his head. "It should end it before it goes any farther."

"There goes that push-pull maneuver again. You can't say the things you've said to me, share what we've shared, and expect me to walk away from you."

"Great sex with a man who's got a target painted on his back, Doc," Joe reminded her with the cold and unpampered outspokenness that was his trait.

She remained silent. Resolute.

"The crazy thing is," he admitted, his voice barely audible, "I'd be disappointed if you did."

It was the most thrilling, most heart-wrenching thing he'd said to her, and she almost sent the tray skidding as she wrapped her arms around his neck. "Then there has to be a way to find out what to do to resolve this," she said with renewed energy surging within her. "If we—Oh, God! How could I have forgotten?"

"Forgotten what?"

"Something J—something he said about an old woman." Feeling Joe pull away as soon as the words were out, she quickly captured his face between her hands. "You *have* to listen, even if you don't like hearing me call him by your name. Last night I didn't pay that much attention because of what he'd said about me, about us. But I remember now. He told me to speak to an old woman. 'The old woman knows,' he said."

"What old woman?" Joe asked, his tone reluctant but curious.

"I didn't know. Not then. He was rambling somewhat, talking about understanding fate or destiny or something. But think about it. Who else could he have meant if not *Jewel?*"

CHAPTER NINETEEN

In the lengthy silence that followed, the sound of old man Bernard's ancient VW revving up and pulling out of the driveway was more like a bus. In fact Joe took so long to respond to Rachel's comment, he wasn't surprised when the light went out of her eyes and she drew back from him.

"What's wrong?" she asked.

"I don't trust her, and I sure as hell don't want you talking to her about any of this."

"It's not as though I'd blatantly—"

"No, Rachel!"

He expected her to argue. She didn't. With a brief, stiff nod, she slid off the bed, snatched up her shirt and left, murmuring, "I'm going to go get cleaned up."

Letting her go was hard, but Joe knew it was necessary. They needed some time apart. Some space. He had to have the opportunity to think, and it wouldn't happen if she was around. Then all he wanted was to drag her back into his bed and lose himself in her softness and heat as he'd been doing most of the night.

God, he was tired—tired of living an existence where he was constantly looking over his shoulder, of not knowing who was harmless and who was dangerous. He was fed up with denying himself almost everything that usually gave him pleasure because it was just too risky, or costly, or unavailable. But most

of all, he was tired of not knowing what was going
to happen.

And as though that wasn't enough, there was the
bridge.

From down the hall came the sound of the bath-
room door closing. The unmistakable hard thud had
Joe slumping back against the pillows and muttering,
"Hell, Rachel."

He'd never been good at relationships. It was why
he'd hooked up with Terri. She hadn't been interested
in anything permanent, any more than he'd been. All
she'd wanted was a convenient bed partner when she
was between assignments—and safety in that convenience. Considering the risky times they were living
in, it had made good sense.

That wasn't to say they hadn't been fond of each
other. He'd put his life on the line for her, hadn't he?
But he'd known the words *love* and *permanence*
hadn't been in her vocabulary, nor his.

Rachel made him think of those words. She made
him think of too many things he had no right to dwell
on.

Hearing the shower water start in the bathroom, Joe
swallowed the dregs of coffee remaining in the cup
and reached for his jeans. As he drew them over his
hips, he heard the sound of an approaching vehicle
and then a shout.

He went to the front window and recognized Mudcat leaning out of his chrome-adorned pickup, which
was glossy in spite of the dreary weather. The front
door opened and Joe recognized a female voice berate
Mudcat for having no respect for "folks still resting."
He'd had to deal with Jewel's humorlessness only a
short while ago.

"Don't know what's wrong with him," she added waspishly. "You wanna know, you go on up and ask."

"Aw, now, I ain't got time to do all that, Jewel. I got me a business to run."

"And I don't? Get going, why don't you, and stop wasting my time."

Joe leaned down to speak through the screen. "Hey." Once he got Mudcat's attention, he lifted his bandaged hand. "I won't be in today."

"You ain't serious? You can't do that to me!"

"Well, I am. Doctor's orders. She says I can't afford to open it up again. Have to watch it for a few days."

"Days!"

From beneath him, Joe heard Jewel's snort. Then the porch door opened and slammed shut again, indicating she'd heard enough and had gone back inside. Good, Joe thought. The less audience he had the better. He shrugged, waved his apology to Mudcat and withdrew from the window.

"Hey...wait a minute!" Mudcat yelled.

It was a risk—he needed the job, especially if it meant he had to stay around here much longer—but Joe didn't respond to Mudcat's call. He didn't want to argue with the guy, and he sure as heck wasn't going to the garage and leaving Rachel here alone. He didn't want to think of how much trouble she could get into during that time.

The sound of Mudcat's truck spitting gravel as it backed out of the driveway drew Joe to the side window. Mudcat happened to look up as he shifted into drive and yelled, "You're finished, hear? Don't you try and come back. And *don't* bother trying to collect any back pay, because I don't owe you anything!''

Then dirt and gravel spat every which way, and the truck shot up the drive. Great, Joe thought, slumping down on the window ledge. Now he'd done it.

He looked toward the bridge and his mood grew more grim. The thing was doing more than bringing him bad luck; it was beginning to give him the creeps. He hunched over and rested his forearm on his knee, studying the swirls of denser mist in the center of the bridge. He still couldn't see anything—he simply wished he understood how, *why* Rachel did.

''I wish the whole damn thing would drop into the—''

A dark flash of movement in the corner of his eye stopped him. He swung his head around to identify it at the same instant the thing slammed into the screen at cheek level.

Joe threw himself from the ledge to the floor and caught his balance by landing with his back to the bed. What the hell? he thought.

Not three feet away, a bat clung to the screen, its claws digging into and bending the wire mesh, its eyes staring at him blindly. Joe didn't know what looked more repulsive—its claws, milky eyes or the intricate pattern of fine blood vessels delineating its widespread, quivering wings.

Grimacing in disgust and wondering what other oddity the weather was going to produce, Joe grabbed up a section of newspaper. Then he struck at the screen one, two, three times. Finally, the creature let go and flew off into the dank, protective veil.

Joe decided he could do without any other nasty

surprises. If he'd been any closer to the screen, those claws could have...

He heard Rachel come out of the bathroom and he went to the door to meet her, knowing she would get his mind off the incident. She looked lovely, fresh and vibrant, her hair wet and slicked back, her face glowing.

"Okay?" he asked, trying to gauge her mood. "That was awfully fast."

"I figured you'd want in there, too. I left you one of my disposable vinyl gloves so you won't have to worry about getting your bandage wet."

Joe thanked her with the same politeness she'd exhibited toward him. Nuts, he thought as she retreated into her room, considering the hurdles they'd managed to champion thus far. It also struck him as a perfect setup, and he stood there for several seconds after she shut her door, thinking how this would be a perfect time for her to get away, make a phone call, search his room, any number of things—if she was of a mind to.

You're a real sweetheart, Becket. Not only absolutely irresistible, but consistent as all hell.

He headed for the bathroom, hoping the sharp spray from the shower would clear his head.

It took an effort, but he forced himself not to rush. He had something to prove to both of them. Drawing the lingering scent of her into his lungs helped, as did taking his time soaping himself down and imagining it was her hands...her mouth.

Enough fantasizing, he decided, feeling himself growing hard. After rinsing off, he shut off the taps, but didn't dry himself right away. Wrapping a towel around his waist, he brushed his teeth, and took more care in shaving than he had in weeks. Finally, deciding he'd killed enough time to prove a half-dozen points to Rachel, he pulled on his jeans again and headed back down the hall.

Rachel's door was still closed. Although he indulged in a fleeting grimace, Joe told himself not to get bent out of shape about it—that is, until he stepped into his room and saw the breakfast tray missing. A feeling of dread weighed down his heart, and he hurried across the hall.

Knocking no longer a justifiable courtesy, he thrust open the door and felt that weight in his heart deepen to his belly. God almighty, he thought, now what had she done?

"Can I talk to you?"

"It's a free country."

Rachel accepted the clipped tone in Jewel's voice as understandable, and determinedly continued across the kitchen. She set the tray on the counter by the sink. "The breakfast was wonderful, thank you."

The older woman stopped slicing the finger-length okra on the cutting board and glanced from the nearly empty plate to Rachel. "If I was you, I wouldn't have shared it with him."

A touch of impishness had a smile tugging at Rachel's lips. "Yes, you would...if you were me."

Something ageless and womanly passed between them. Jewel's eyes twinkled briefly, and then she snorted. "Don't know why I have a soft spot for you, senseless as you are. You'll end up bringing trouble to this entire house." She tipped her head in the direction of the swinging door. "He know you're down here?"

"No. He's taking a shower, and I do need to get back upstairs before he worries."

"That one don't worry about much."

They could go around and around on the subject of Joe and possibly end up agreeing, Rachel thought, not unwryly, but there wasn't time. "I came down to ask you about something."

Her expression must have exposed some of her deeper distress, because Jewel's shrewd eyes narrowed with interest and caution. "What's the matter? Can't find the answers in your fancy medical books?"

"Let's not argue," Rachel entreated. "I'll admit I've looked upon what you do with more than a little skepticism, but I think you might be the one to resolve this problem."

Jewel sniffed. "You don't overdo the sugar, do you?"

Recognizing she'd won her point, Rachel continued, "What would you say if someone's response to a question I posed about the future was—" she paused to get the phrasing correct "—'There's only what is and what will be'?"

"I wouldn't say nothing until I lit me a half-dozen white candles." Jewel put down her knife and turned to Rachel, wiping her hands on her apron. "What've you got yourself into? Who told you that riddle?"

"I can't tell you." When Jewel's dark eyebrows drew together in a threatening scowl, Rachel knew some careful footwork was in order. "Please, don't ask me for names or specifics. Isn't it enough that I was told—No, that's not exactly right, either. It was insinuated that you would help."

"Ahh…"

Jewel crossed herself before reaching up into a cabinet for an old cup and saucer and carrying it to the stove, where she poured a half cup of dark, grainy liquid that resembled old coffee or undrinkably stout tea. Rachel hoped whatever it was, it wasn't for her.

"Sit," Jewel directed. "Drink."

Rachel sat, but was resolute about the rest. "Thanks, but I'm not really thirsty."

"You want my help drink."

She hoped the results would be worth it because the stuff was putrid. Rachel tried her best to get as much down as she could without gagging, all the while wondering what it could possibly have to do with her question. Finally, unable to bring herself to deal with the silt in the last inch or so, she pushed the cup away.

"Turn it upside down."

"What? Why?"

"Do it. Upside down."

About to refuse, Rachel glanced up at the pantry where the curtains shifted subtly. No, she thought, fighting the clammy hand of fear inching across her shoulder blades and around her throat. Lowering her eyes to the cup, she quickly turned it over onto the saucer. Then she glanced toward the pantry again.

The curtains were still.

Idiot, she thought. Her imagination was going haywire because of a draft.

Jewel sat down opposite her and drew the saucer across the table. Her wide, flat lips were compressed in the familiar, stern line as she picked up the cup. The expression changed the moment she looked inside, and a faint keening sound rose from deep within her.

"What?" Rachel asked, her heart thudding again.

"Life and death. Life and death." The woman's normally husky voice carried a sing-song quality and she rocked back and forth, her eyelids drooping.

Then, abruptly, she put the cup down as though she couldn't bear to touch it and leaned toward Rachel. "Listen to me now. You're the life-giver." She pointed up toward the ceiling. "That one's the harbinger of death. Y'all be on a collision course that wasn't supposed to be. Mmm," she moaned, "powerful bad. Powerful."

"What do I do?" Rachel heard herself ask. In the sane recesses of her mind, she knew if anyone like Sammy heard her say that they would have her committed, but once the question was out she felt relieved and hoped that Jewel could tell her something that would end the confusion and fear that was beginning to take control of her life.

"No powders or charms for this. This is bigger than black magic."

"Bigger?"

"Life lessons always are," Jewel continued, her eyes wide now and hard in their stare. "Look for what's before your eyes. Be true to what's in your heart."

"You're not saying anything!" Rachel cried in frustration.

Before Jewel could answer, the swinging door crashed open, hitting the wall. Joe stood holding it there, his chest heaving.

"The soulless one," Jewel whispered. Hastily

crossing herself again, she collected the cup and saucer and dashed to the sink.

Joe ignored her, his eyes boring into Rachel. "Upstairs," he ordered.

CHAPTER TWENTY

The hardest thing for Joe, as he followed Rachel up one flight of stairs and then the next, was dealing with the temptation to do violence. Because it had been born of panic. Because the reasons for that panic couldn't be more ill-timed and potentially catastrophic.

Not until they reached the third floor did he trust his disciplined side enough to look at her. But seeing her watching him with those soulful, doe-eyes nearly undid him all over again.

He'd fallen in love with her. Maybe he had been in love all along and had only been psyching himself into believing it was simply lust. Whatever the case, he knew it would be easier to face the barrel of a gun than to have to cope with the conscious acceptance of his feelings.

No, he had no time for this, and he wanted to be angry with her for once again making him aware of that, furious with her for making him ache to his heels with wanting her. He wanted to hate her for making him think as a man and not a machine. Oliver was right for saying he didn't need enemies because he was too good at being his own.

"Will you let me explain?" Rachel asked softly.

"Do yourself a favor and don't say a word, not one word, or by heaven I'll...do something for the sheer relief of getting it over with."

She walked directly to his room. Grateful for not

having to touch her to get her there, Joe saw his un-
made bed with the imprint of their love-sated bodies
still visible in the twisted sheets, and it mocked his
relief. He slammed the door to purge at least a modicum of his frustration, and began pacing from one
end of his self-created prison cell to the other.

"Why are you being like this? You knew I was
coming back."

Did he? Then why had he felt as if some clawed
hand had ripped a hole in his chest and torn out his
heart?

"If I hadn't brought that tray down, Jewel would
have come back upstairs for it."

"Don't use day-school logic on me," he warned,
his tone low and deadly. "You went down to talk and
for no other reason, so can all that common-sense-
with-a-dash-of-good-samaritan bull."

"All right!" she cried, spreading her arms in acceptance or surrender. "What if I did? I was only
trying to help! Again! Why do you have to react as
though I've committed some impossible offense?
What have I done that's so bad?"

He laughed, he swore, he wheeled around, grabbed
her and gave her one hard shake. "Wake up and look
at me. I'm a walking corpse."

Rachel's face turned ashen. "Don't say that!"

"Why not? It's what you've been trying to convince me of, only from a different perspective. But
my version is the scarier version, Doc, because mine
doesn't try to avoid reality. There's no hocus-pocus
solution. No black wax, voodoo doll or other stupid
junk is going to change the facts.

"I've lost everything I've worked for, and there's
a good chance that all I have to look forward to is a

bullet from Maddox or one of Garth's other thugs. The last thing I need is to be burdened with the worry that they'll take *you* out with me.''

He only realized what he'd admitted when he saw her expression go from bruised to beatified wonder. Dread and remorse shook him to his core.

''You don't suspect me anymore,'' Rachel whispered.

''I suspect everyone.'' Especially himself, he thought bitterly. Especially his sanity.

''You care!''

''I didn't say that, either.''

''No,'' she agreed. ''You're too noble to burden anyone with the words. But you can go ahead, growl and protest all you want. I've heard enough and I've stopped listening.''

Her eyes turned soft and dreamy. Her mouth... ''Damn it, Rachel,'' he groaned.

He could no more keep from dragging her against him or seeking her mouth, than he could stop breathing. Once her scent was inside him, he wanted more, and he reached deep seeking it—everything— the way a man who'd lost his world would reach for heaven.

His mouth still locked to hers, he gasped for air. Never would he have believed that even in the pain of his truths he could find such pleasure. As Rachel responded without hesitation and gave herself wholly to his next kiss, as she'd done with the first, it was all he could do not to drag her down to the hard floor. He wanted her, him, without clothes. Closer. Immediately. And all the while she met his unchanneled passion, his blind demand, with acceptance and encouragement. Words were unnecessary, yet he tried to give her what he could. "I want... Never like this, Rachel. Never."

"I want *you*," she whispered in return.

Her breathy response made him feel like his legs were stuffed with nothing more substantial than saw-dust, and shot his control into some black hole of oblivion. Afraid, almost angry, that she might not un-derstand, he dropped back against the closet wall he'd felt behind him and lifted her flush against his aching hardness to let her know it had been no idle comment.

She proved equally concise. Wrapping her arms more tightly around him, she slid a leg up along his to his waist.

He groaned. They were racing for trouble.

"I mean it," he warned.

"Mean it."

"Like this?"

"Please."

He spun them around to push her against the wall. There was a thud from inside the closet, one that dragged a muffled oath from him, but when she de-manded he ignore it, he did. For about three seconds he thought about carrying her to the bed; for as long as it took for her to wrap her legs completely around him. Then he abandoned the idea. The mussed bed was too civilized for the wildfire igniting between them, anyway. He would give her what she wanted...for as long as she wanted...until neither of them could move, let alone worry about what the next hour might bring.

But mutual agreement could be hell on intentions and style and grace. Joe discovered that when their hands suddenly tangled at the buttons of her blouse. His solution was to clutch the material and rend it in

two, abandoning even that as soon as he had access
to her. Discovering she wore nothing underneath had
fueled his eagerness, and he quickly ducked his head
and closed his mouth over her right breast.

Rachel gasped, a shudder of ecstasy leaving her
momentarily limp in his arms. Then her fingers, short-
nailed and small-boned, but defying the limitations of
either, bit into his shoulders and tugged at his hair.
When he suckled harder, she writhed and bucked
against him, a strangled moan rising from deep within
her.

He thought her sounds alone could drive him over
the edge, but then she began to whisper his name,
over and over. It roused some demon from the prison
he'd sentenced it to.

"Joe...*Joe*...Joe..."

It wasn't supposed to happen again. He'd championed his doubts, his jealousy over whether she was
caught up in him or something she wanted to see. Or
so he'd believed.

"Look at me," he demanded.

She did, and her eyes were bright with fever. It
released his own and, impatient, he grappled with her
jeans, dragging them, everything, down. Loosening
his own things, he spun them around again, using the
wall for balance as he lowered them to the floor.

They united in one fluid surge, their gasps of pleasure merging as did their breaths and their tastes. But
it wasn't enough.

"Look at me," he demanded again, and when she
did he entreated, "Don't stop."

"It can't last."

It didn't have to, because nothing should feel this
good, not when it also kept total happiness hostage.

Fortunately, his body didn't give a damn about philosophy and principle. Feeling the tide of spasms swell and claim her, it surged toward its own release.

She could barely breathe, and the heat was edging toward unbearable again, yet Rachel rested her head against Joe's shoulder and nuzzled closer to lick at the beads of moisture along his freshly-shaven jaw. She knew he didn't want to hear it, but she ached to tell him that she loved him.

As though he could read her mind, or at least sense something, he trembled. After a few moments he mumbled, "Do you suppose there was something in that omelet or the coffee?"

Sensing that he needed a moment of lightness, Rachel teased, "You mean you're not usually a relentless wildman at this disreputable hour of the day?"

"Doc—" he took a second to catch his breath "—this might come as a shock to you, but until you came along, sex was just that. Maybe an outlet for stress, I'll give it that, too. But I sure as hell never found it as crucial as my next breath."

Needing to see his expression, Rachel lifted her head and searched his face. He needed sleep. There were deepening lines of fatigue at the corners of his eyes and beside his mouth, but the glint of possession was clear and made her heart overflow with love, tempting her again.

Joe quickly shook his head. "Don't do it. You don't know that you mean it and I don't want to hear it."

"Why not? You told me what you were thinking."

"No. I told you that I wanted you—a fact that isn't going to have any effect on anything I have to do."

As quickly as it had come, her happiness was snatched from her. Determined not to be defeated, Rachel used the hem of her ruined blouse to blot the sweat from his creased brow and above his upper lip. The movement bared her breasts again and drew his gaze in a way that made her clench inner muscles to torment him in return.

He sucked in a sharp breath. "Witch."

"No. Just a woman who's discovering what it means to feel completely desired for the first time in her life. No one's ever made me want to abandon control before."

"Rachel…"

She knew he wanted to resist touching her, but she took his hand and moved it to her breast. "Please. Just for a few minutes, can we act as though we have all the time in the world?"

"But we don't."

The words were brief, his tone clipped, and even though he kissed her hard, he also managed to get them both to their feet. Crisply excusing himself, he adjusted his clothes and walked out, heading for the bathroom.

What did you do with a man who resisted the force of the winds and the pull of the tides…everything to reach his own destination. His resolve became her pain. As she fumbled with her own clothes, finally tying her buttonless blouse at her midriff, she had to fight against the urge to feel sorry for herself and fear for them.

Stop it, she ordered herself. She punched the flat of her fist against the closet door, disgusted that her tear ducts chose now, of all times, to want to flow.

Inside the closet, something responded to her mild

blow. It reminded her of the sound she'd heard earlier.
Curious, she opened the door and saw a video tape
box at her feet.

She couldn't believe it. Where had he been hiding
it? She looked up and around, finally noticing a shelf-
like ledge she hadn't noticed before above the door.
Yes, she thought, stepping inside the closet, the box
must have been up there when he bumped against the
wall.

For all the care and hesitation she exhibited while
picking it up, the box might as well have been a poi-
sonous snake. Nor did she care for the way it felt in
her hands. Why should she, when it was the bane of
Joe's life? The only thing to do was to get it back up
on the shelf before he returned.

Then again, why should she? She had nothing to
hide from him, certainly not the fact that she'd seen
it—especially since he must have heard it fall down,
too.

She set the tape on the bureau, just as she heard
his step behind her.

CHAPTER TWENTY-ONE

Rachel turned to find Joe pausing in the doorway. He looked from her to the tape and back again, the expression on his face masked by a familiar blankness she had begun to recognize. He always relied on it when he was gauging a situation that looked incriminating.

"It fell from the shelf in the closet. You must have heard it yourself," she added when her initial comment didn't seem to have any effect. "I didn't want you to think I was trying to deny being aware of it, so I left it there for you to put away."

From the side window came Adorabella's childlike soprano, fussing about how the weather was keeping her patio tomatoes from ripening. At the front window a squirrel and a blue jay were arguing over territorial rights to a certain branch. They were sounds of normalcy that should have been reassuring, but only emphasized the silence inside the room.

Finally he sighed. "Guess I wasn't as clever at hiding it as I thought."

"Oh, I wouldn't say that," she replied, eager to reassure him. "Don't forget, I didn't see it when I was snooping around for your ID."

His answering look told her he would rather forget that episode, and he crossed over to the bureau for the video. A part of Rachel wished she could view it, but she knew what Joe's answer would be if she asked. It was just as well, though; there wasn't a VCR in the house that she knew of. And if they were able to find one, no doubt it would be impossible to keep Jewel or Adorabella from trying to catch a peek. She decided having Joe's trust was more important.

"Would you like me to go to my room until you find a new place to put it?"

Indigo turned to sapphire as amusement lit his eyes. "I guess not."

"Better be careful. I might take that to mean you're beginning to have faith in me."

He let his gaze wander downward, taking in the way she'd tied her blouse. Passion—so much a part of him it pulsated below the studied calm—flared briefly before he championed control again. "Let's say it's simply that I don't see a reason for either of us to leave the premises for a while, in which case it can stay in here."

He opened the top drawer of the bureau and set it inside. But his comment started Rachel wondering again.

"Don't you have to make a call or something to let your boss know you definitely won't be in?" she asked.

"Trying to get rid of me, after all?"

"No! It's only that yesterday you sounded some-what...vague about how things stood between you two."

"Yeah, well you can relax about that, too. He was by earlier while you were taking your shower."

His droll tone left her feeling dubious rather than reassured. "Why don't I like the sound of that?"

"Maybe because he fired me."

"That's awful!" This added pressure he didn't need. "What are you going to do?"

"Hope that Garth makes his announcement when the media's been reporting he will. It's only a few more days."

A few more days. Rachel knew she'd heard that sometime during conversations with patients or Sammy, but then the news had no impact on her life and so she hadn't paid much attention. She wished she had; in fact, she wished she knew a whole lot more about Gideon Garth and his connections. For once, her aversion to everything political was showing her that she'd as good as bit off her nose to spite her face.

"What about you?" Joe asked, breaking into her thoughts.

"You mean my job?" She shrugged and slid her hands into her back pockets; she didn't think he needed to see her fidget, which was what she felt like doing. *A few more days...* "I guess I'd better try going back to the clinic on Monday and grovel until Sammy lets me have my shift back. That is," she added pointedly, "if you're no longer considering me a hostage by then."

Joe reached out, hooked a finger into one of the front belt loops and tugged her toward him until they were close enough to kiss. "I'm beginning to wonder who's the hostage to whom?"

"If it's any consolation, I don't know, either."

"It's not."

She touched his cheek. "I only want to see you safe, Joe."

"You think I have a death wish?"

"Of course not." But he did have the spirit of a

rebel, and that, combined with his intelligence and vitality, made her fear he'd channeled his energies toward something that could harm him while he tried to help others. In other words, he had the stuff of which heroes were made; that was always terrifying for those who had to sit on the sidelines and watch. And she'd never been a good spectator in the best of times. "I can't help wishing you could think of another way to handle this."

"Believe me, I've considered them all. There isn't."

"You could change your mind and give them the tape."

He released her as though she'd turned into something to be shunned, and walked to the front window. "How can you even suggest that?" he muttered, his back to her.

"Because I think what you're planning to do is tantamount to throwing your life away." Rachel came up behind him, ran her fingers over his tense right trapezius muscle and, feeling it twitch, withdrew her touch. "This can't be the only solution. There has to be another way to buy you time to mount a different, stronger case against Garth and the group he's involved with. Please, give this a thought...I have a few contacts of my own in Washington. Not many, but good people. Once Garth announces his candidacy for the U.S. Senate, I can talk to them and they can prompt an inquiry."

"I've seen Washington's idea of an inquiry," he replied, his tone scathing.

"They're not all like that. Anyway, the point is that you'd be alive to carry on other work. The work you were meant to do."

"I was meant to take down slime like him and Maddox, not turn my back on their brutality in order to save my own skin."

"But there are so many Garths out there," Rachel insisted. "I can't believe—I *won't* believe—he's your only dragon."

Joe turned to face her, his expression steely. "Would you have let anyone ask you to forget what drove your brother to take his own life?"

"No," she admitted, momentarily lowering her gaze because she knew he'd made a major point. "But I'm not asking you to forget anything. I'm asking you not to get yourself killed."

This time she was the one who turned away. Knowing she needed something to do before she lost control completely, she went to the bed and began straightening the sheets. She felt when Joe turned to watch her, knew when he came to stand directly behind her. Straightening, she accepted his touch as he took hold of her shoulders.

"We always come back to the bridge."

"How can we not?" she asked, feeling as though invisible hands were stealing the happiness they'd briefly shared, dragging it deep into the mist to leave her barren and cold. She was grateful when Joe began massaging her shoulders and rubbing her arms.

"What's on your agenda for tonight? What time will you go back?"

He hadn't said, *Are* you going back?—as though to remind her that her choices were dependent on his consent. She tried to take some satisfaction from that, but it was fleeting and slight in the face of everything else. "I don't know that trying anything would do much good. He was so weak last night. I'm not sure

I'd be able to see him at all tonight, let alone communicate with him.''

Joe's hands stilled. "Do you realize you said 'he' this time, not 'you' or 'me'?''

"I know you didn't like it when I did that. Oddly enough, you seem more alike now than when I first met you both.''

"Just what I wanted to hear,'' he muttered.

"I meant it in the best way.''

"You mean I'm not quite the bastard you thought I was?''

Rachel leaned back against him and covered the arms wrapping around her with her own. "It helps to know it's not easy for you to keep me at a distance.''

"I'm not.'' When she tried to spin around and face him, he tightened his arms, keeping her still. "Don't go all bristly—you know what I mean. The lower my defenses get, the more potential there is to make the wrong decision if something unexpected comes up that puts you in danger.''

She had no time to bask in even a second of joy at those words. A commotion outside had both her and Joe hurrying to the side window. As they reached it, a crow rose from the lower branches of the towering oak nearest them and returned their startled stares with an unblinking one of its own.

On the ground, Jewel shook a broom at it and shouted, "Evil creature. Get away!'' Then she broke into a tirade of gibberish Rachel could only guess was voodoo spell-casting. The bird, however, remained unimpressed and continued to gaze at her and Joe.

"Isn't he a strange one?'' she murmured. "As much as they like scraps, the crows usually avoid getting too close to Jewel's kitchen door.''

"You think *that's* something, you should have held off on that shower a few minutes," Joe replied. "A bat hit this screen like an addict zeroing in on his junk."

Noticing the claw marks he pointed out to her, Rachel made a face. "That is odd. They usually retreat from daylight, don't they?"

"You call this daylight?" Joe muttered, just as Jewel picked up a stone and threw it into the tree.

"No more tapping on my window, hear?" she warned. "Take your black heart out of here. Go!"

Rachel had difficulty breaking away from the crow's mesmerizing stare, but she managed. "Jewel? What happened?"

"The devil's been tapping on the kitchen window."

"What's wrong with that?"

The housekeeper's expression reflected pure horror. "Means death's coming to visit this house. Get away from there now. Don't let him fix his eye on you."

But he already had.

Rachel backed into Joe hard, almost sending them both toppling. At the same time, Jewel threw another rock at it, this time skimming the bird's chest. The creature spread its wings and took flight, drawing a relieved, if spontaneous, breath from both Joe and Rachel.

"Well, who needs television with all this entertainment?" she said with an embarrassed, nervous laugh. "I'd hate for Sammy to have seen this. He'd never let me near the clinic again."

After a slight hesitation, Joe replied, "Oliver would have shot it."

Rachel wasn't sure she'd heard right. "What?"

"He's real superstitious. It comes from being raised by his grandmother, a real mean old broad who kept him in line by scaring the crap out of him. She had a pet chicken she supposedly used for casting spells on neighbors and people she didn't like, and for his fourteenth birthday—because she wouldn't let him go hang out with his friends for the day—he gave himself the present of borrowing a pal's python and putting the chicken and the python in his grandmother's bed."

Poor little boy, Rachel thought, wondering about such anger-driven boldness. "That was risky, though. She could have fainted from the shock!"

"Oliver said she did, right after she killed the snake and methodically cleaned up the place. But she retaliated, too. She swore he'd hexed her. And he said that afternoon a crow came to her window and started tapping. She told him it had come for her soul. Oliver was so scared at the idea of being blamed for that, he went and shot it."

"That's unbelievable."

"Yeah. I can't believe I'd forgotten it."

"Did his grandmother survive?" Rachel asked, not sure she wanted to know.

"Heck, yes. She even quit bullying him so much. But he did have to give up JV football and get a part-time job to buy his friend a new snake. I never could convince the old lady that if it wasn't Harvey *I* didn't want it."

She would have laughed had she heard this at any other time. It was a funny story, perfectly capsulizing how strong individual willpower was in overcoming the most bizarre of circumstances. But instead Rachel sat down on the edge of the bed, torn between bewilderment and dread. "I think I may be losing my mind, Joe. I can't decide whether to be afraid of what's happening to us, or sorry for remembering I've never had a pet. Not in my entire life."

CHAPTER TWENTY-TWO

Joe knew he would spend the rest of the morning brooding over Rachel's words. This was exactly the kind of thing he couldn't afford to hear at this stage. His life was in shambles, there was a good possibility he wouldn't get to celebrate his thirty-sixth birthday, and he'd realized he'd fallen for a woman who might also be falling in love with a ghost. But all he could think of was Rachel as a raw-hearted child who'd grown up learning how to hide her loneliness and pain, until some clumsy-tongued cop broadsided her with reminders of it. It brought him dangerously close to wanting to hear more, to talking about his own failures and fears, to making promises about how they would have the chance to do things he had no business making promises about.

He managed to get past the first impulses of protection and tenderness by making an offhanded excuse that he'd forgotten to go downstairs and pick up the newspaper he had delivered to the house.

By the time he returned upstairs, Rachel had recovered. He saw it when he realized she'd not only finished straightening the bed sheets, she'd retreated to her own room.

"I have some correspondence to catch up on," she told him.

She held up a sole letter. The lamest of excuses. It did, however, tell him that not only did she live as

frugally as a nun, but she kept her relationships down
to a spare few, as well.

He withdrew to his own room wondering who the
letter was to—specifically, if the recipient was female
or male, and was it a friendship or more?

Then he saw the headline on the front page of the
paper: Garth press conference Monday at White
Mills. After that even his jealousy had to take a back
seat.

Monday…which meant it would all be over sooner
than he'd expected. Adrenalin surged, and relief,
along with a sense of finality. Three days. He'd hoped
the event was going to take place minutes from here
at the Garth homestead, but White Mills had the
courthouse, and he could understand Garth's wanting
a suitable backdrop for all those cameras that would
be focused on him.

Afterward he forced himself to read the rest of the
paper, even the ads, in an attempt to get his racing
thoughts and emotions back under control. Not only
didn't he want to waste energy getting wired too
early, but there was no use in adding to Rachel's distress. Unfortunately, the parish's journalistic effort
was a modest offering, and it wasn't long before Joe
found himself pacing again.

"Want some company?"

Barefooted, Rachel proved a dangerous woman.
He'd lost track of how long he'd been at his post by
the front window, but Joe hadn't heard her moving.
Finding her in his doorway would have been disturbing if his emotions weren't more keyed in to admiring
the picture she made standing there.

"Sure." The reply was automatic, but as he let his

gaze sweep over her, he wondered at the wisdom of
the invitation. She hadn't changed out of her blouse,
and that snug knot at her midriff did nothing to keep
him from glimpsing her touchable skin or appealing
shape. "Get your letter done?" he asked, shifting as
his body roused.

"No. I started it several times, but I couldn't finish.
Too many things hanging in the air."

"Yeah, I know what you mean." He'd finished his
first cigarette of the day not ten minutes ago and
found he had to consciously resist having another for
the same reason. "Is it to an old friend?"

"Almost the oldest, considering you can count my
relationships on two hands and still have fingers left.
She's my ex-roommate, an up-and-coming sound editor in Hollywood. I guess all those hours of watching
horrible movies with her are paying off."

"It's hard to think of you being close to someone
in Hollywood."

"You mean the cellophane image?" Rachel's first
response was a crooked smile. "Quinn would surprise
you. She's the most down-to-earth person you'd want
to meet. Has a brain like a turbo-drive computer and
the sense of humor of a mortician. Her only two
weaknesses are movies and her hair."

"I can understand the movies if she's in the business, but what's the deal about her hair?"

"It's incredible. The color, the texture…a mink
would kill to have it. Whenever it grows down as far
as her backside, she sells a hunk of it to some makeup
artists. She says, last count, the stuff's been in five
movies."

Joe didn't know whether to be amused or what. But
before he could think of a proper reply, Rachel spot-

ted the paper he'd put on the nightstand. He'd neglected to mix it with the rest.

"You don't want to look at that," he warned, regretting that the few moments of lighter conversation was about to come to an end.

She hesitated. "Bad news?"

"Depends on how you look at it."

"Try from your point of view."

Soft voice, gentle persuasion…she would be good at the subtlety game. But he was tired of games. "It's going to go down sooner than I'd anticipated, Doc."

The last traces of light went out of her eyes and she picked up the paper, found the article in question and lowered herself onto the edge of the bed. "Monday…" she whispered. "So soon."

"Guess I got myself fired just in time," he offered with false cheerfulness. He shouldn't have bothered; he could tell she saw through it right away.

"I'm sorry, but I have to ask one more time. Isn't there any way to talk you out of going through with this?"

"No." He saw whatever hope she'd managed to remuster extinguish in her eyes like a candle flame in a gale wind. "I'm sorry, Rachel, but my decision's final."

"They'll kill you."

"It's a possibility. They might do that no matter what I did or didn't do. On the other hand, maybe I'll be home free."

Her expression turned incredulous. "What do you think has been going on out there this past week? What do you think I've been risking my sanity—my entire *career*—trying to comprehend and then prove to you?"

"Lower your voice," he warned, although he hated having to make the rebuke.

The breath swooshed out of her, and she curled her legs into a lotus position as though folding into herself. "All right, but don't expect me to sit here quietly and let you destroy yourself."

"Rachel..." What? What could he possibly say to her at this point? "Look at it from a rational point of view. The press conference is scheduled for 10:00 a.m. on Monday in White Mills. That's where they'll try to get me, because that's where the tape will be. Not on that bridge out there in the middle of the night. For that to happen they'd have to know where I am, and if they knew where I was, they'd already have been here, wouldn't they?"

The hint of a wobbly smile lifted the left corner of her mouth. "Sure."

His own expression warmed. "Try to take reassurance in the thought that if I'm able to tell you that much, it also proves I trust you, doesn't it?" he added quietly.

Rachel started to rise from the bed, then stopped, as though unsure of herself or him. But the moment he extended his arms, she ran to him and wrapped her arms around his waist, pressed her cheek against his bare chest and held on. Hard.

Having her so close again had an abrupt and profound effect on him, both in a physical and emotional sense. Yet even though he slipped his hand beneath her hair to caress the back of her neck, his heart remained heavy with regret as he realized that no matter how many more moments like this he was given, they wouldn't be enough to fill the void of an eternity without her.

* * *

Rachel didn't try to respond at first, she simply tilted back her head to study him. This week's extra stress was beginning to get to her and she knew it showed on her face. She even had to keep her lips compressed more than usual to stop them from trembling at the most unsuitable times.

"You're scaring me, Joe, and I hate to let fear take control of even a small part of my life."

"Then you should understand why I'm taking the position I am better than anyone," he replied urgently. "I can't allow myself to accept all that's been happening around here the way you have. If I did, I'd have to acknowledge, then deal with, the fear, all the probabilities of failure. An army of one can't open itself to that kind of suppositioning, Doc."

"So you think ignoring the odds makes more sense?"

"I'll bet plenty of people went out of their way to tell you how you couldn't get through school on your own, that what you were doing made no sense either. But you went and did it, anyway."

"That was different." Rachel stepped back so she could think clearly. How could he compare the two? "I'm not going to be overmodest and say what I did was easy, but it was hardly a matter of life and death."

"That's overmodest, Doctor Gentry." Joe tilted up her chin further. "People have crumbled like sandcastles under less pressure than what you've heaped on yourself through the years."

"Even so, what you're involved in is far bigger. This is your *life*."

"It's my *job*."

Who did he think he was kidding? Job! He couldn't

stop being a cop any more than she could take a break from being who she was. A sense of finality overcame her and Rachel rested her hand against her stomach as she realized what conclusion she'd come to.

"What's wrong?"

"I think breakfast may not be agreeing with me."

"Ah...honey." He put his arm around her and turned her toward the bed. "You don't deserve my foul mood. Why don't you lie down?"

"No. I think I'll go ask Jewel for some ginger tea."

"That sounds more like punishment, not a cure."

"It soothes indigestion better than anything I dole out at the clinic." Rachel eased away from him and headed for the door. "I'll be back in a few minutes."

She took the first set of stairs like someone who truly was feeling unwell. In case he felt he should follow, she cautioned herself. But once she reached the second floor, she broke into a dash, her bare feet moving lightly down the polished steps.

Once she reached the foyer, she glanced back up the center of the stairwell to check upstairs again. From upstairs came a sound. Footsteps.

She backed a few steps out of sight and listened. The footsteps were more like shuffling, and the blowing of a nose identified the person more clearly. Not the third floor, but the second. Old Mr. Bernard was on his way to the bathroom, which meant he was back in from his morning checkers game with his cronies and was about to take a nap before lunch and his afternoon game of dominoes at the café.

The man sounded like a foghorn, Rachel thought, shaking her head. She used to wonder how Celia Nichols could sleep through all that—until Adorabella told her how Jewel had found earplugs in Celia's room, along with a sleeping mask.

Once things settled down again, Rachel went straight for the phone in the cubicle beneath the stairs and dialed for information. A few moments later she dialed the number the recorded voice had given her.

A female voice answered on the third ring, and Rachel asked for her party. Less than a minute later, she found herself listening to an all-too-familiar drawl.

"Hello…?"

She could barely make herself reply. "Mr.…Mr. Maddox?"

"Yes? Who is this? You sound familiar, do I know you?"

"That's not important," Rachel replied. "I know you."

Their conversation went surprisingly smoothly and was agreeably brief. Just before she hung up, Wade Maddox said, "Hey, sugar, come on. Tell me your name. You know I'm gonna find out, anyway."

Carefully, she set the old-fashioned receiver back on the cradle of the phone.

There, she thought, it was done.

Backing away from the phone, she felt something cool and breezy. But spinning around, she found nothing.

Disconcerted, she went to glance into the parlor. It was empty. Adorabella, who often liked to sit in here at midday hoping to catch Mr. Bernard before he slipped out, was, no doubt, still in the kitchen with Jewel fussing over that crow. At any rate, it had to be her subconscious that had made her sense the presence of an eavesdropper.

She started back toward the stairs again and realized it was too soon. Joe wouldn't believe she could have made and drank the tea so quickly. So she decided to go into the kitchen and beg Jewel for a beer for him. It might help keep him from asking too many questions.

In the dining room she saw that either Adorabella or Jewel had replaced the roses in the crystal vase again. These were a deep crimson red. Bloodred. Rachel frowned, not able to recall having seen that particular shade anywhere around the property.

Well, there must be a bush she'd missed, she thought, pausing to touch one of the petals, because dew still clung to them. She rubbed the moistness between her fingers and thought how lovely, but tragic somehow. Like her mood. Like her future.

Then she noticed it wasn't moisture she was smearing between her fingers at all. It was blood.

CHAPTER TWENTY-THREE

Joe decided he'd had plenty of time to think about what he'd said to Rachel and that he couldn't take any of it back. But he also knew he wanted to spend what time he had left with her. So when she returned from downstairs, more pale and subdued than before, he was more quick than usual to tune in to that.

"I think you're coming down with something," he said, crossing over to touch her forehead and cheeks. "It's as I thought, you have a slight fever."

"No," she said quickly. "It's just the tea."

But when she stared at her free hand for a moment and then, abruptly, began rubbing her arm as though she was chilled, Joe wasn't convinced. "Rachel... you're not well."

"I'm fine," she insisted. "And you know what? Instead of worrying about me, we should be looking at your cut and changing that bandage."

Joe didn't buy her sudden show of cheerfulness for a moment. "It'll wait. Why don't you lie down and try to rest for an hour or two?"

"No! I mean...I couldn't sleep right now. Besides, I want to be with you."

It was what he wanted, too; so much so that hearing her say the words filled him with pangs no other hunger could hope to match. It amazed him that he managed to plant an almost benign kiss on the tip of her nose, and he smiled. "I want you with me, too. How about using my bed? Maybe we'll both end up taking a nap. Considering how much sleep we've been missing lately, that might not be a bad idea.''

"Drink this first.''

He accepted the beer she handed him, touched that in her condition she'd thought of him. To placate her, he took a long drink, then urged her onto the bed. But he didn't lower himself beside her until she insisted he stay close.

"Comfy?'' he asked, once he adjusted the pillows against his back and had her curled against him.

"Thanks. But maybe this is too hot for you, even with the fan on.''

He'd relented and switched on the noisy relic, thinking it might help her. "Doc,'' he drawled, hoping to win a smile from her, "in case you haven't noticed, I stay hot around you.'' He didn't get the smile, but he did enjoy the way she rubbed her cheek against his chest.

"Tell me what you were like as a boy, Joe. Were you as clever at getting girls to do what you wanted?''

"Hardly.''

"I don't believe that.''

"They thought I was too arrogant.''

"That must have hurt.''

"Not really. I was too busy having fun to notice.''

"I'll bet your mother thought you could do no wrong.''

Joe took a long swig of beer and thought about all the ways he could answer that. "My parents divorced when I was nine. We were never a close family. The court gave my mother custody of me, but she didn't really want me around—especially not after she hooked up with Phil. She finally let me go live with my father when I was eleven.''

"You mean, you didn't get along with your step-father, either?"

"He and my mother never married, and I never thought about him as any kind of father figure," he replied, feeling as though he was talking about something from another lifetime.

Rachel sighed and stroked her hand soothingly up and down his torso. "It sounds as though you had it rough."

"I was fine once I got back to my father. You would have liked him, Rachel, and he would have…" He'd almost said, "loved you, too," and it would have been one of the most natural things he'd ever said to anyone. That revelation, along with the awareness of the short time they might have left, made him take another deep swallow of beer.

"He's gone, isn't he?" she murmured, sounding almost awkward, as though she understood what he was going through and felt it, as well.

"Yeah. About two years ago. It was during a drug-related murder investigation. He was the detective on the case and while tracking down a lead he got in the middle of a domestic argument. In our business it's one of the most dangerous scenarios to find yourself in, and in his case it was unexpected."

"That's tragic."

"It happened less than a year before his retirement. He'd planned to move to Galveston. All he wanted was to fish and drink beer until he got fat enough not to get into trouble for watching the girls go by in their string bikinis."

Rachel made a sound that could have been a chuckle or an empathetic sigh. "The theory being that fat men are safe?"

"Yup." Joe couldn't help but grin. "But he would've proved it unreliable."

"A lady-killer like his son, huh?"

Bemused, he frowned, shifting slightly to see her better. "Is that how you think of me?"

With eyes shut and a faint, sad smile curving her mouth, she replied, "No matter what you said about yourself, the first time I saw you, I felt such a... You don't need to hear that."

Joe put the beer on the table beside him and tilted Rachel's chin up, forcing her to look at him. "Tell me. I want you to."

"Awareness. I felt as though you were reaching straight into my soul and..."

She trembled and buried her face against him. The movement was reminiscent of how she lost control when he made love to her, and Joe drew her closer because he had no choice, he needed to. But inside he couldn't dismiss the nagging reminder that technically he wasn't the one she'd met first.

He swore silently.

"I'm sorry. I know you don't want to hear that, and I have no right to burden you with my rambling nonsense when you have much more important things to focus on."

Her gentle words deserved some reassurance, some thanks, but caught in his own nightmare, Joe found himself unable to provide them. He didn't, however, want to relinquish his hold on her, either.

"Shh...you need to shut down and stop carrying the world on your shoulders for a few hours. Close your eyes. Go on. I'll be here when you open them."

For a moment he thought she might argue, but then

she relaxed, curled more securely against him and let the compelling tide of fatigue carry her away.

It was better this way, he thought, ignoring his body's tenseness. As it was, he wouldn't make it to Monday without taking everything she offered him, but at the moment he had just enough nobility left to keep his hands to himself.

But he yielded on his other weakness and reached for the cigarettes beside the bed. To hell with resolutions, he thought. There was little doubt in his mind that a bullet would stop him far before any damned cigarette could.

With every breath, fog seeped into her lungs, filling them until, too late, she realized she was suffocating. She fought for oxygen, but it was everywhere, and spreading...extending like fingers covering her head, closing around her throat, covering her mouth. Cruel, punishing fingers full of malice and mischief.

She had to move. She had someplace she had to be...yes, a meeting, and she had to find the strength to struggle and fight.

Somehow she broke the fog's phantom hold over her mouth and throat and pushed onward across... Oh. It was the bridge.

Joe—that's why she was here. She was going to see Joe. Energized with the thought, she surged forward and fought harder, needing to reach him.

Lights stopped her. Lights that came from behind. There were two, sudden ones, twin beams in the middle of the road like those from a car. It had crept up behind her and abruptly turned on its high beams. Wondering why she hadn't heard the car coming, she shaded her eyes to see who would be so callous and cruel.

She heard a door open, and footsteps. "Who are you?" she demanded, her voice sounding foreign to her, heavy like the fog, deep like the darkness, and fearful. Not her voice at all, she thought. What was wrong with her?

A man stepped before one of the lights, becoming a silhouette instead of simply a voice. His size made her nervous, though. Big, brawny, and it disturbed her that she couldn't see his hands.

"Hello, Rachel. I understand you have something for me?"

She looked down and realized she held a box in her hand. She hadn't noticed it before. Was she supposed to give it to him? Why did that seem wrong? Yet she didn't think she wanted to keep it herself. That didn't feel right, either.

"Why do you—?"

A flash stopped her. She heard a roar and then she was flying…flying backward. No, falling. And she couldn't breathe.

She landed hard on the wet road, dazed and terrified. Then the pain came, slow, steady and building until it was horrible, burning and relentless. It ate at her like a carnivore. She clutched herself around the waist and tried to twist away, but every inch took incredible strength, too much. What's more, the man was advancing.

To her horror, he pointed a stick at her. Wrong— wrong, not a stick…the barrel of a gun. At her forehead.

"Oh, God, don't! Don't hurt me anymore!"

"You deserve this, Rachel. You know you do."

"No. I only wanted to help. To save him!"

"You can't, but don't worry. You'll be together soon."

She heard him pull back the trigger, and she screamed again. "Joe! Joe!"

She tried to sit up, but hands held her down. She fought, struggled with all her might and wept because she couldn't get free. "Oh, God, please. Don't do it. Please don't..."

"Rachel, stop it. It's me!"

In the vague blue-white light she saw the half-moon face of the man looming over her. She saw how he held her by her wrists and how her hands were clenched painfully into fists, how her whole body was shaking with rigidity and terror.

But she was alive.

Joe was alive.

It hadn't happened. Yet.

CHAPTER TWENTY-FOUR

"You were having a nightmare, Doc."

She'd figured that out herself—a nightmare that had been going on for days now, with this chapter being so real Rachel couldn't stop shaking.

"It was only a bad dream," Joe continued soothingly, as he slowly released her wrists to draw her into his arms. "Take a deep breath. Good. Try another one. You'll feel better in a minute."

She already did, in a way. In another way, she knew she would never feel normal or right again. She tightened her arms around his neck. "Don't let me go."

"I won't."

"Stay with me."

He made a strange sound deep in his throat that could have been a laugh. "You're with me, sweetheart."

Confused, Rachel glanced around and saw she was, indeed, in his room, not hers as she'd first thought. She also noticed, casting a resentful glance toward the window, that it was dark. Late. "What time is it?"

"Almost eleven-thirty."

She hadn't believed she would sleep so much, and for so long.

"What?"

He had a frown in his voice, one she knew she couldn't avoid with an indifferent reply. She tried, anyway. "I didn't know it was so late."

They'd napped earlier, and later in the afternoon Rachel had gone down to talk an increasingly recalcitrant Jewel into preparing a tray of potluck for them. Afterward, Joe had tried—not too successfully—to get the news on the TV. The reception couldn't have been much worse, but they got to hear another report on Gideon Garth's upcoming announcement. A splashy, overblown version, since the colorful state senator was rivaled by few people for flaunting his uniqueness, which played best in the visual media.

Joe had turned off the set as soon as the story concluded. They'd tried to carry on a conversation; it hadn't worked any better than the TV did.

Rachel couldn't remember falling asleep. She would have considered it a blessing if it hadn't been for the nightmare...and the hour.

"You're getting tense again."

"I'll be all right in a minute."

"You want to talk about it?"

"No."

"Are you sure? It might make you feel better."

"Trust me. It wouldn't."

He seemed taken aback by her bluntness, or more accurately, her rudeness. She understood and sympathized with what he must be feeling, but she couldn't explain. Not now. And later...later he probably wouldn't want to listen.

"I'll be right back."

As he left the bed, Rachel reached for him. "Where are you going?"

"To get you some water. Do you want me to bring your bag for some aspirin or antacid or something?"

She'd forgotten she'd blamed her previous mood

on an upset stomach. "No. Nothing. Not even the water. Don't worry about me, just stay."

She barely had hold of his fingertips. Then she won his entire hand, his arm…and finally, he was back down on the bed and looming over her.

"Rachel…" Joe shook his head and brushed her hair away from her forehead. "You're too used to being independent, do you know that?"

"It's better that way. You can't afford to worry about me. And I have no right to ask you to."

"Since when did you start selling yourself short?"

"Since I decided not to waste the rest of our time together being a liability to you."

Joe had turned the fan off before he'd turned on the TV, and the only sounds were nocturnal ones from outside. Plus her heartbeat thudding in her ears.

"Do you know you're the most unusual woman I've ever met? No matter what happens—"

"No, don't talk about it." She turned her head away in secret anguish. This was the one thing she couldn't bear.

She thought any other man would have misread that, accepted it and retreated—rather, let her leave, since this was his room, she reminded herself again. But then, she'd known too many people who quit too easily; the world seemed full of them these days. Her mistake was not remembering that Joe Becket wasn't one of them.

"You're right," he said after a studious moment. "Besides, words would hardly be adequate for what I want you to know."

And then he forced her to turn back toward him and took slow, thorough possession of her mouth in a way that silenced any further need for dialogue. It

was a kiss from a man who'd clearly been counting
the hours, maybe the minutes, before he could do it
again. The kind of kiss that neither asked nor apologized, but simply, honestly, boldly *was*.

He explored and tasted her as though it was the
first time, and then expanded that journey of discovery to her lips, her chin, her throat and her ear. Rachel
became a creature of reflex, tilting her head back, to
the side, arching her neck. Whatever he wanted, whatever she needed, she gave and took because her heart
thrummed a devastating message beneath its excited
beat: *this was the last time.*

The scent of urgency was held captive by the night,
and yet what neither of them did was rush. Seconds
after abandoning a kiss-sated spot, they explored it
anew. By the time Joe had returned to her mouth a
third time, Rachel knew her lips would stay tingling
and swollen for hours.

As though they'd made some pact, neither of them
spoke, but their communication remained constant
and acute. Rachel knew the instant Joe wanted more,
their bodies unhampered by clothes and free to explore without interruption. She knew exactly how to
shift, leaning back and letting him trail kisses down
her throat again, while his skillful fingers journeyed
over her full, hard breasts to the knot keeping them
apart. Then it was undone and he was peeling the
cotton off her, sliding his hands under her and lifting
her to his mouth.

She wanted—needed—this. It was her last gift to
herself, and more—the punishment she deserved for
all the tomorrows she would never have. *They* would
never have. Reality hurt, and she wanted to feel every
second of it.

He finished undressing her. No one had ever done that to her before. For her. It was exciting. Debilitating, she amended, realizing she'd lost the ability to do the heretofore simple mechanics on her own. He worked like a surgeon, serious and efficient, only to surprise her by suddenly lingering over a curve here or a mole there. Then she was exposed to the night, the heat and him.

Although she saw only glimpses of his face, she could also *feel* the way he looked at her, and it made her want to cry. She didn't deserve it, and in that instant knew she would choose death before having to see his regret over having exposed this wonder and adoration.

Aware she was dangerously close to tears, she survived by trying to focus on getting his jeans off. It should have been simple, she thought with a flicker of her old amusement—the man remained an exhibitionist around her. She should have been able to handle three more inches of zipper, but nothing was simple when Joe Becket was aroused. In the end he had to help her, and by the time his jeans were kicked off the bed, the mystical light caught the faint sheen of moisture glowing on both of their bodies.

For a moment they experienced the singular pleasure of lying side by side with only a whisper of contact—breast to chest, thigh to thigh, palm to palm. Man to woman. Then he gently urged her onto her back, slid downward and placed a kiss just below her navel. Her breath caught in her throat and she went completely still.

The sheets whispered with his movements, and the next kiss landed on her right thigh.

She trembled. "Don't," she whispered, her heart beginning to pound furiously.

He made no reply except to award a twin caress to her left thigh. And then she felt his thumbs stroke upward from those places.

Rachel reached down to stop him.

"Why?"

"I can't."

It wasn't the response she'd intended to make. She'd planned to say, "Because," or "Not tonight," or even "I don't like that." She hadn't expected terror to win a coup over control and make her voice crack. It stole everything from her and laid bare the truth. And Joe knew how to deal with truth.

He simply laid his cheek against her thigh and stroked his five o'clock shadow, six hours older and that much more virile, against her already tingling skin and whispered, "I need all of you tonight, Rachel. I need to feel whole and alive. Don't say no."

His honesty and vulnerability defeated her. Her desire overpowered her. Like a moonflower unfolding to the mysterious advance of the moon, her body yielded and blossomed.

She felt the caress of his breath first, then his mouth, and always his heat. He sent her quickly to a sharp peak, and even more skillfully to another. She thought she would die from the pleasure and nearly did shatter from the love. And needing to return that wonder in kind, the moment he began to rise over her, she quickly pushed him off balance and rolled him onto his back.

"Rachel...you don't have to."

"Yes, I do."

He trembled at her whispered insistence. It filled

her with joy and gratitude and determination. Then the room fell quiet again, as she began bestowing on his body equally sensual caresses.

She'd never done this to anyone, and yet loving Joe was the most natural thing she'd ever known. When at last she touched him as intimately as he'd caressed her, he uttered a hoarse groan and then blindly buried his unsteady hand in her hair.

All-new emotions spawned to life within her. She was gratified to know she could move him so deeply, and yet surprised at discovering how giving regenerated her own excitement, so that when he gripped her arms and dragged her over and beneath him, she was ready.

They came together quickly, smoothly, and the blue-white light of the moon had never been hotter. Rachel folded herself around Joe and watched hunger grow fierce. His face was breathtaking. Even as the power of his possession created an almost devastating strain, she refused to close her eyes. She wanted to see him in his moment of ecstasy, imprint his image on her memory forever. They were so close, so attuned, she could almost swear they shared one heartbeat. She wanted to remember this instant of bliss and prolong it. Perfect it.

As though he could read her mind, Joe linked his hands to hers. Then, sliding them over her head, he intensified their union to that last degree and gave her that perfection. Rachel felt herself stretched and sensitized beyond comprehension, only to surge beyond it as rapture claimed her.

Joe went still, rigid, pulsating inside her, but his gaze held her gaze as powerfully as his hands gripped hers.

"You're mine, Rachel."

"I know it."

"And I'm yours."

Tears kept her silent, but she knew he could see them shimmering in her eyes.

"It's timeless, Rachel. Nothing and no one can change what we've created. Timeless."

Then his voice broke, as hers had done before, and under the relentless power their joining had created, they rode their wave of bliss together.

It took a long while for heartbeats to calm. Rachel relished each one, and Joe's peace.

"You'll sleep now," he whispered in her ear, his voice growing thicker from satisfaction and the lure of sleep.

"Yes," she replied, her eyes wide open.

"God, Rachel..."

"I know."

"What did I ever..."

"Hmm?"

"...do to deserve you?"

She kissed his strong, square chin, praying he would succumb quickly before her resolve gave out. Finally he did, and her eyes stayed dry because some tears only poured from the heart.

CHAPTER TWENTY-FIVE

Rachel listened as Joe's breathing deepened. When he rolled onto his back, she began the careful, slow maneuvering to ease out of bed.

He seemed at least partially conscious of their broken contact. Barely seconds after he'd settled in the new position, he sighed in his sleep and shifted restlessly.

Rachel froze and waited...until his breathing steadied once again. With an internal sigh of relief, she continued her cautious maneuvering.

By the time she was completely out of the bed, the clock on the nightstand read nearly 1:00 a.m. At the rate she was going, she would be cutting things close, and that left her with very little time for mistakes or unexpected problems.

She dressed focusing on speed and silence, not neatness; there wasn't much she could do with her shirt at this point, anyway, she thought, tying it back the way she'd been wearing it. Then she tiptoed to the bureau. It was more like step, listen and step. If she sensed even the possibility of a board yielding under her weight, she paused and shifted over an inch or two. She'd spent a good portion of the day trying to learn where the weak boards were in the room, hoping that Joe had only seen a woman tense and pacing from restlessness.

No, don't think about him. You'll start making mistakes if you do.

Her years of developing her patience worked to her benefit, because once she got to the bureau, she had to wait for Joe to make a loud enough movement to cover the soft sound of opening a drawer. It took so long that by the time he did mumble in his sleep again and roll over, she had to abandon her plan to shut it, after she'd taken the tape.

The distance from the bureau to the door seemed like the Grand Canyon at first. But she painstakingly championed it, as well, even if her hand was soaked with perspiration by the time she put her fingers around the doorknob.

As she looked over at Joe one more time, her heart pounded painfully against her breast. She yearned to touch him and kiss him one last time, but she knew it was impossible.

I do love you. I only hope that someday you'll understand how much...and then forgive.

Feeling as though she were leaving a part of herself behind, she cautiously stepped out of the room.

"Rachel...?"

She almost dropped the tape, almost failed to check a startled cry, almost had a heart attack. Grateful for the darkness that hid her attire, she forced herself to poke her head back in the door and whisper, "What?"

"You okay?"

"Yes. Go back to sleep."

"Where're you going?"

He sounded mostly asleep, and that gave Rachel back some of her confidence. "Bathroom," she replied, her own voice hushed, soothing. "I'll be right back."

She heard him mumble something and shift to find

another comfortable position. After a moment, he drew in a deep, contented breath and drifted under again.

Faint with relief, Rachel touched her head to the doorjamb. That was more than a close call, she thought. That was nearly the end. She decided it wouldn't be a bad idea to turn on the light in the bathroom in case he awoke again and glanced out of the room to check on her. Maybe it would buy her some crucial minutes.

Once she did that and shut the bathroom door, she was set for the stairs. With the boxed video and her sneakers in one hand, she grasped the railing with the other and decided on her first step, her second, her third.

By the time she got to the second floor, the muscles in her calves and thighs were cramping. But she knew she could relax somewhat. Correction, she thought, speed up.

Once she arrived downstairs, she sat down on the landing, relieved to have to take a minute to put on her shoes. Her pulse rate was going at a sprinter's speed and her body felt as though it had run a marathon. Then she heard something that made her forget aches and pains.

Yes, she thought, lifting her head, there it was again…a creak, like a door opening somewhere in the house. Silence followed and held. Not a closing sound, not any footsteps, just those two instances of brief intrusion on the night's calm.

Had someone heard her? Who? Because she'd had her head down she'd missed details, and, too, the acoustics in the house had always been bad.

What if it was Joe?

What if it wasn't Joe?

She thought about all the other sounds she'd been wondering about since moving in...and the roses that had been pulled from the vase...the petals that had stained her fingers with blood, only to vanish like Joe's blood had vanished on the bridge.

She couldn't deal with this. Hastily finishing with the laces on her shoes, Rachel bolted for the door. Once she was outside it would be all right, she assured herself. She had to concentrate on the priority at hand. No matter what, she was going to save Joe.

Except the damn door wouldn't shut. The dampness, she realized, was finally having an effect on it, the same way it was permeating everything else. Not now, she commanded with an inner groan.

Tucking the tape between her knees, she used both hands to try to tug at the door and yet not slam it— an impossible task, she soon discovered when the wood gave and a thud resounded around her. Horrified, Rachel held her breath and waited.

Joe came awake like a flipped-on light switch. At first he hadn't a clue as to what woke him; much faster came the realization that Rachel wasn't beside him.

Where'd she go?

And how long ago had it been?

He vaguely recalled their having a brief dialogue, and guilt rose, bringing with it shame. What if she was feeling badly again? What if she was seriously ill? She'd been subdued, even tense, for most of the day, not that he'd been Joe Cool.

One thing was for certain, he thought, shifting his legs over the side of the bed, he wouldn't get back to

sleep until he had her back in his arms. Considering
the mess his life was in, it spoke profoundly of what
had happened to him, of how *she* had changed him
to where he could nod off as though he didn't have
a care in the world.

He opened the door and immediately saw the glow
of light from beneath the bathroom door. Rather than
reassure him, it deepened his concern. Too long, he
thought, wandering down the hall. And he didn't like
the quiet.

He hesitated outside and then knocked softly.
"Doc? You okay?"

She didn't answer.

"Rachel?"

A cold dread crept up through the floorboards into
the soles of his feet. Before it could reach the back
of his neck, Joe had pictured a half-dozen hideous
images and was stepping away from the door, bent
on racing to retrieve his gun. Then he stopped, for
the first time in his life frozen by indecision.

Indecision? That's Rachel in there.

Swallowing, he gripped the doorknob and swung it
open.

Brass hit wood. Light spilled into the hall. But
there was no sign of Rachel.

He couldn't believe it. His brain didn't want to help
him figure it out, either. Acting on pure reflex, he
hurried down the hall and threw open the door to her
room.

Empty again.

No, his heart told him.

Think, his mind demanded.

But she wouldn't have gone downstairs. Not with

the bathroom door closed. Open, maybe, to guide her way, but not…

He swore.

The bridge. That goddamned bridge. If he could, he would tear it down or blow it up himself.

He dashed back to his room and snatched up the clock. It was getting close to that time. "Damn," he muttered, striding to the side window. That's when he saw the opened drawer.

As a bitter taste formed in his mouth, he forced himself to go look. It was gone.

And you believed all you had to worry about was competition from a ghost.

Joe ran to the window. It was no use. The fog was as thick as the mud pie they served at the café. If she was out there, she had a perfect protection and one helluva head start.

He couldn't believe it. She'd actually done it. No wonder she'd paced around here all day like a frantic caged animal. And he'd believed she was sick.

She'd been counting the hours until she could betray him! Even her lovemaking was probably a sacrifice to the good of the cause.

Well, she wasn't going to get away with it, he told himself, snatching up his jeans and dragging them on. Jerking open another drawer, he pulled out a T-shirt. Once she found out she didn't have—

Joe froze. In the next instant, he lunged for the closet, switched on the closet light and dropped to the right corner where he moved his duffel bag out of the way. Digging his knife out of a rear pocket, he lifted two boards that he'd found worked loose when he'd first moved in.

There was the real tape, safe and sound. So she

hadn't known he'd set up a ruse. At least he could be grateful for that, he thought, struggling for crumbs. But her boss wouldn't be thrilled when he played what she brought him and discovered it was nothing more than the soap opera Oliver's wife had taped for herself while at her office job.

Which meant they would be coming to get him soon.

He had to get away.

Listen to yourself, man. You're that willing to believe everything you shared with her was a lie?

What else could explain what was going on?

With tape in hand, Joe went to retrieve his gun.

Think about what she'd said earlier. Think about what you said. You've both been taking risks on faith all along. She's no more out to cut your throat than you'd be able to pull the trigger on her if it came down to it.

He groaned, thinking about what that could mean. Could she be risking her life for him?

It would never work. They would kill her for the pure pleasure of it, just as they would kill him.

"Sweet Jesus, Rachel," he muttered, and scrambled for his athletic shoes.

He ran down the hall and took the stairs by storm, not giving a damn who he disturbed or offended. Since he had no idea how much of a head start she had on him, he couldn't afford to waste any more time.

At the base of the stairwell he nearly ran headlong into Jewel. The old dragon looked even more spooky without her turban. Her hair was white. Loose, it flowed like fine wires past her shoulders, floating up and down with the slightest move as if live electrical currents were flowing through it.

"Call the police," he demanded.

"You leave her be," she replied, crossing her arms. "It's good she's got herself out of this house and away from you. And if you don't leave her alone, the only thing the police are gonna be called for is to put you away where you won't be doing nobody no more harm."

"I don't give a damn why you call them, lady, just do it! Tell them to get to—" *Where, damn it, where?* "—to the bridge," he said, not sure why the words came out of his mouth since he'd been thinking elsewhere. "Tell them there's a riot or something going on. Hell, I don't care what you tell them, but get them up there!"

"Why?"

That brought him up short. He spun around, ready to read her the riot act for not being able to see the obvious.

Why should she? You're not doing so great yourself.

"Because I love her!"

With that, Joe raced out the front door, his gun in the waistband of his jeans and the tape in his bandaged hand.

Outside, the fog was every bit as thick as it had seemed from indoors. The densest yet. Joe could barely see ten feet in front of him, let alone the bridge. Only a faint glow from buildings and security lights gave him a hint as to where he was going.

Not giving a damn, he charged down the driveway and up the dirt road toward the main street, wanting badly to call out to Rachel in the hopes that she might stop. But he couldn't risk it. There was always the chance that he was already too late, that she wasn't alone. Worst of all, what if, like last time, he found he couldn't get onto the bridge?

He was about to start up the incline when lights made him drop to the ground. A car eased past him. He was able to make out only a few details, but they were enough. It was Maddox.

CHAPTER TWENTY-SIX

"Hello? Is anyone there?" Rachel called cautiously as she approached the center of the bridge.

She glanced back over her shoulder, toward the direction she'd come, but didn't see or hear anything. She hoped that meant she'd been imagining things and that Joe wasn't following her...or anyone else for that matter.

There was no sign of Wade Maddox, but then she'd said two o'clock and there were still a few minutes to go. It had been a crazy hour to insist on—Maddox had been very annoyed—but she'd held firm. She was glad, because she was hoping to see her other Joe one more time, to tell him that she finally understood and what she planned to do.

Her other Joe.

Realizing how she'd formed the thought made her wince.

Maybe after tonight it wouldn't matter so much that she'd never completely managed to reconcile their separate identities in her own mind. All that she needed to know was that she'd found justice for the two identities, so the Joe who was doomed to this bridge wouldn't have to suffer anymore...and so his living counterpart wouldn't have to die.

God, just thinking about it all got her confused.

"Rachel."

The voice was the most ephemeral of whispers. It

didn't matter, though; she would have recognized it anywhere.

"Joe!" She spun around. "Where are you?"

She felt a presence; she was able to distinguish that for certain, but no more because she also became aware of a vehicle approaching. Squinting, she saw twin lights on some dark form easing up onto the bridge like a creature of prey. Was this it? she wondered, stepping out into the roadway and protecting her eyes from the glare with the videotape.

It stopped a few yards away from her, close enough for her to recognize it, but not the two people inside. However, she could guess—Wade Maddox and his sidekick had arrived for their appointment.

The driver didn't turn off the engine. Rachel didn't know if that was good or bad. The passenger door opened, saving her from having to worry about it, and Maddox stepped out. She squared her shoulders, determined not to let him know how frightened she felt.

"Well, well," he said, his drawl laced with humor and sarcasm. "Dr. Gentry, you are one surprise after another."

"Mr. Maddox. Thank you for meeting me."

"Oh, you're very, very welcome."

Because of the headlights, she couldn't see his face. It put her at a disadvantage. There were undertones in his voice that made her increasingly nervous. "Before I hand this over to you, may I ask you a question?"

"Only if you'll let me ask you one."

He was laughing at her again. It annoyed her, but she suspected that was the idea...and that he didn't expect her to do much in retaliation. It made sense, since she figured both he and his partner were carrying a gun. So far they hadn't seen fit to show any weapon, and she preferred to take that as a good sign—until the thought came to her that they might want more than the tape.

"I wanted a reassurance, actually," she told him. "Do you mean to keep your promise about dropping the matter of Detective Becket?"

Maddox lifted boxy shoulders in a negligent shrug. "If what you're holding proves to be authentic, then I don't see why not, ma'am."

"You can take my word for it that it is."

"Well, I'd like to do so, ma'am—Rachel—but this is a bit more complicated than what you and I would prefer."

Rachel felt a sinking sensation in the pit of her stomach. "Would you care to expand on that, Mr. Maddox?"

"Now don't get all bent out of shape. I'm merely talking about what would be fair for both parties."

Fair. She was getting fed up with that word. "And exactly what is it you want?"

"To view the tape. If it's legitimate, we've got a deal."

"How do you propose we do that?"

"It's quite simple. You come with us to the senator's home, and we'll check things out there. If everything's in order, we'll bring you straight back here."

Back to explain to a man who wouldn't want to listen, she thought grimly, but replied, "Of course it's in order."

"Then there's no problem." He stepped aside and opened the back door of the car.

Rachel knew she was way out of her depth here.

She didn't have a clue as to what to do, what risks were worth taking, but she also didn't think she needed to have a gold shield to sense she was in danger. "I'd like to wait here, Mr. Maddox."

"Uh-huh...well, that's not how it works."

His voice took on an edge she thought was as sharp as the toothy smile she remembered. It made her all the more certain that she wasn't going to get into his car. "You don't understand," she said, raising her voice while also stalling for time and trying to think. "I'm not a part of whatever it is this is all about. I really don't know the details."

"Why do I find that hard to believe?"

"I only know you want *this*," she said holding out the tape. "And you're welcome to it, but that's all. I've never viewed it myself. I'm not involved with whatever it is that your argument with Detective Becket is about."

"Good old Becket... You know, you didn't mention where he was."

Rachel's tense leg muscles started to tremble. Where, she wondered with no small dread, was one of those damned eighteen-wheelers when you needed one? "I don't know."

Wade Maddox hung his head and laughed dryly. "Rachel, Rachel, you should've stuck to medicine, honey. This definitely isn't your area of expertise."

"Which is why I'll be extremely grateful if you'll take this and go."

He didn't answer right away. Instead, he took a few steps toward her and, drawing his gun, aimed it at her heart. "Get in the car," he replied, all humor drained from his voice. "Now."

She thought she'd experienced fear before, like

when Joe bullied her in the bathroom that first night—
was it only three days ago?—and then the day after
at the garage, and later when he cornered her in his
room. This, she suddenly realized, was much worse.

But could she give up? "I—" she swallowed
"—I don't think you'll use that."

"You're wrong."

"I told someone where I was going."

"No, you didn't. Now get in the car, because I'm
tired of messing with you. And if you don't move,
I'm going to aim at your kneecap to make it hurt
more. Then I'm going to throw you over the side of
this damned bridge and let the snakes and gators have
you. There's not much meat on your bones, but I
don't reckon they're fussy, do you?"

"Try that and the tape comes with me," she replied, amazed she could get the words out. "In which
case, you'll never know if it'll be found by anyone
or not."

"Don't play chicken with me, lady," he growled,
taking low aim. "I don't scare."

There was a strange shift in the wind. It swirled
the fog, creating shapes and shadows around them.
And then Rachel heard it, the two very different
sounds, as different as a whisper was from a crack of
thunder.

"Rachel…"

Two sounds, yet one voice.

Joe.

And Joe.

She stepped aside and tried to see behind Maddox,
who'd spun around, having apparently heard it, too.
Some yards away the fog became a figure—legs,
arms, head, but transparent…and a few more yards

back, the mist parted and he was there again solid, bold and very much alive.

As they both charged Maddox, the more vivid Joe gained ground on his vaguer image, came closer, and closer. Could he see him? Rachel wondered, frozen in awe and terror. What would happen if he caught up with him?

Abruptly, she knew. As Wade Maddox raised his gun and took aim, she knew with a terrible clarity that had her screaming in protest.

"No!"

Oh, God, what had she *done?* How could she not have seen it sooner? With her common sense and logic, she'd still failed to see what was before her eyes.

"There's only what is and what will be."

"You can't help being you."

"He won't be able to resist you, Rachel."

"You've got to understand your own life lessons."

She'd interfered. Insisted on getting involved where she had no place. Worse, she'd forced Joe to change his destiny. She'd taken his choices away from him and had replaced them with her own.

And the price for all that was death. His.

Full clarity in the space of a heartbeat.

No, she thought, lurching forward. Not if she could help it.

It all happened like a film stuck in slow motion. She threw herself at Wade Maddox to ruin his aim just as the two Joes met. Merged. The instant it happened, she saw the more vivid of the two faces register shock and realization.

Then she was caught up in her own survival. Maddox was far too big for her, and he threw her off him as though she were nothing more than a jacket he'd shrugged off.

She hit the street, a sharp pain streaking up her arm, momentarily blinding her. At the same instant a shot rang out.

She stopped breathing. Was it only wishful thinking that made her believe she'd seen Joe throw himself to the right at the moment Maddox fired? There was too much light flashing in front of her eyes, but the fog remained to distort and confuse.

Another shot blasted the night's stunned silence. This time Rachel screamed.

Wade Maddox reared backward, past her, and crashed to the street.

His driver stared at the still body before glancing dazedly at Rachel. She waited for him to pull a gun and kill her. Instead he floored the accelerator. The sedan took off across the bridge with both the driver and passenger doors hanging wide open.

The sound of sirens seemed wishful thinking at first. But suddenly there were lights, too, overhead red and blue lights identifying two squad cars. The vehicles swerved, shutting off the sedan's escape.

The car's brakes screeched, creating smoke that rose to meet the mist, and the car slid sideways for a length before coming to a halt.

And then there was silence. It was over.

Out of necessity rather than thought, Rachel took a shaky breath. Because he was so close, she forced herself to glance at Wade Maddox's still body. He was dead, his eyes wide and staring up into the night, the expression of disbelief frozen forever on his face.

Having seen enough, she struggled to her knees. She needed to get to Joe. She didn't know if she could bear to go through with it again, but maybe, she thought, maybe this time she could help him.

To her amazement, he reached her first.

She stared up at him in mute wonder. He stood straddle-legged before her, chest heaving from belabored breaths, his face an unreadable mask in the blue and red lights. As he had been on the previous days, he was dressed in the white T-shirt and the jeans. But one thing was different—there was no blood.

"You're not shot," she murmured inanely.

"No. Not for lack of trying. I guess the fog messed up his aim. And you. If you hadn't screamed...jumped him..." He looked away. "I don't know."

Was that what made a difference? Did she dare believe it? What did it matter except that he was alive. *Alive.* She could bear anything now, even his disgust with her for being willing to betray him, and to let him walk away.

But he didn't walk away. He fixed his gaze on her again. "You've got a lot of explaining to do."

She nodded, tried to get to her feet, but found her legs wouldn't hold her. Exhausted, she sat back on her heels. "I know. Believe me, I know. But if it's any consolation, I'm sorry if I made you think I was—"

"You did," he confirmed, his curt reply full of bitterness.

She couldn't bring herself to look at him, afraid to see the revulsion come. "I didn't know what else to do. I thought your life was worth more than that tape, that maybe later you could figure out a way to expose Senator Garth without endangering your own life. I was being selfish."

"Yeah."

"No one has the right to interfere in a decision as important as this one was to you."

"No."

This was going to be even harder than she'd expected. Pent-up tears made talking difficult. "I wouldn't blame you if you wanted to prosecute me or something yourself."

"The thought of some form of violence crossed my mind," he said, sounding too agreeable. "But then I thought about what Maddox would do to you once he found out you didn't have what you thought you'd had."

Confused, Rachel shot a look upward. "What?"

"That tape's a fake placed to fool anyone snooping around in my room. The real one was better hidden. Realizing that you didn't know that and how angry it would have made Maddox made me sick to my stomach, Rachel." Joe dropped to his knees before her. "Do you think I would have let him touch you?"

She was going to collapse from relief and happiness. "You don't hate me," she whispered in wonder.

"It would be a lot simpler if I could. What you did was dangerous, stupid and dead, *dead* wrong, but... Ah, jeez, Rachel," he groaned. "Come here."

She flung herself into his arms and held on for dear life, absorbing his trembling as he absorbed her. But it wasn't enough. For him, either, she learned a few seconds later when he began covering her face, her throat, her hair with desperate kisses until she was dizzy with their combined passion, so dizzy she barely felt the gun he still held crushing into her back.

"I love you. I love you. I love you," she cried over and over.

"Don't stop saying it."

Never, she thought, grateful for him to even want to hear it. She wouldn't let him know that it hurt a little not to hear it back. It was enough to be held, to be wanted, forgiven. And then she glanced over his shoulder and remembered the seconds before he'd shot Wade Maddox. The night looked different now, and she knew why. A deeper sadness filled her.

"What is it?" Joe asked, leaning back to study her face.

She didn't get to answer. From behind them came the sound of running, a cautious pause, and then a man said, "Put the gun down, son. Real slow."

CHAPTER TWENTY-SEVEN

"They had to call in the FBI," Joe explained to her in a hushed voice as she sat stiffly in Adorabella's parlor and watched the two men talking across the room with one of the policemen who'd been at the scene. "This situation falls under federal domain."

"They all look and act like clones," she replied ungenerously.

Ever since they'd arrived from their office in Baton Rouge, they'd done their best to keep her and Joe apart. She'd especially disliked how, once they'd found out who her parents were, they'd offered to call her father for her and get her on the next plane back to the East Coast. They'd said, "I'm sure your minimal part in this can be handled through the Washington office, Miss Gentry." And their eyes had been alight with the hope that their care would garner them at least a letter for their files.

"It's Dr. Gentry," she'd corrected, and had left them to Joe ever since.

She'd spent much of the time apologizing to Adorabella and Jewel for causing so much commotion at this hour. The entire Nooton police department was here now. Mr. Bernard, too, having drifted down in his robe looking a little dazed but interested. In fact the only person missing was Celia Nichols—not that anyone had found that a revelation.

What had been fascinating was watching Joe handle the other law enforcement people. They'd wanted

to establish an impression of authority from the beginning—and to let him know in no uncertain terms
that his maverick behavior wasn't amusing in the
least. Most of all that he'd nearly given Gideon Garth
and his affiliates a straight shot to freedom...and
more power.

Through it all, Joe held firm. "I've done my job,"
he said coldly. "You do yours."

The two of them hadn't had an opportunity to talk
much in the past three and a half hours, but that coldness had seemed to transfer itself to her whenever she
felt his gaze. She wanted to tell him he needn't worry,
that she would cooperate in every way she could, and
that she wouldn't let anyone know he'd threatened
her at one point...or that very soon afterward they'd
become lovers. Wouldn't everyone have a field day
with that information? In a way she couldn't blame
them; it hardly seemed sane to her.

A week—three days, actually—and they'd gone
from being strangers to intense intimacy. Of course,
it was strange. She didn't even know when his birthday was. And what was his favorite food? Had he
ever made angels on a beach at dawn?

But she did know he'd been trying—and succeeding—in the most desperate days of his life to give up
cigarettes. That he liked to watch her when he thought
she didn't notice. Sweet heaven...that he liked to fall
asleep with his hand covering her breast. Not much
of a life preserver, she thought as the phone shrilled
again.

Joe crouched before her, but was careful to avoid
any contact. "They want us to go to Baton Rouge.
Depositions and stuff. And...okay, I won't lie to you,

they think we'd be safer there. Even though they'll be picking up Garth soon, he has his supporters.''

''Do you want me to go?''

''We either go willingly or unwillingly.''

''Do *you* want me to go?''

''I know this is going to add to your problems at the clinic...''

His tone was apologetic and patient and nothing like what she'd heard since the first moments after life had gone upside down on the bridge. ''I'll have to call Sammy,'' she said, adopting a matter-of-fact tone herself. ''And it'll only take me a few minutes to pack. But you know that, don't you?''

She made the call. As she expected, he was already at the clinic. When he learned what had happened, he wanted to come over.

''No, don't. We're leaving in a few minutes, anyway.''

''I feel like a pig. Why didn't you tell me?''

''It was...complicated.''

''When will you be back? *Will* you be back?''

She hadn't thought of that and relied on her new standby—''I don't know.''

''Look, Rachel. We'll work around it. If you need time, you've got it. If you want a transfer, you've got that, too. I just wish I'd guessed the magnitude—''

''Sammy, you've been the best.'' She felt tears rising again and had to cut the call short. ''I'll talk to you as soon as I can.'' As soon as she hung up the phone, she raced upstairs.

She needed space, privacy from the boring eyes, and to pack.

But once in her room, she began to shake again. It

wasn't a reassuring sign. Brutally, she dug deep and demanded control.

She would get through this. She would do and be all Joe needed her to be, and then she would worry about getting her own life back in order.

Light from the window drew her. She walked to it, noticing it would be dawn shortly. A different dawn this time. The sun would rise over Black Water Creek Bridge, turning the sky pink and lavender, then orange and finally gold. The fog was dissipating. It was wonderful news except that its passing meant someone she'd grown very close to would be going, too.

Her door opened. She quickly went to the nightstand and checked a drawer, knowing full well she'd never put anything there.

"Are you all right?" Joe asked, shutting the door softly behind him.

"Sure. It won't take me a minute."

"Do you need to talk? To ask me anything?"

"No. I'm fine."

But he obviously wasn't convinced. As she headed for her closet and her suitcase, he stopped her.

"You're no more fine than I am." He drew her into his arms and pressed his cheek to her hair. "You're exhausted and confused and worried what the future holds, because we came to some edge of the world a few hours ago. Rachel...it's changed us forever."

Unable to keep from yielding to her need, she held him as she longed to. "We can't tell them about the bridge and the fog, though, can we?"

"No. No, we can't."

"Then tell me. You saw him, I think. In the end, you saw him, didn't you?"

"Rachel..."

"Didn't you?"

"Yes. And I'll never admit that again to anyone, Rachel, do you understand? Because I can't. Except to you."

It was enough. It had to be enough. "All right."

He went still and seemed to sense her strange mood. Stepping back slightly, he studied her soberly and asked, "Why does it feel as though you're slipping away from me?"

"You're tired."

"I love you, Rachel."

She hadn't been expecting that. Considering that a few hours ago it was all she'd been hoping to hear, it gave her hope.

"Do you understand what I'm saying? Wanting?"

Wanting? This time she had to shake her head. "No."

"I have no right to ask you to change your life again after all you've been through. I don't know what trouble it could raise asking for a transfer, considering I'm not even sure *I* still have a job or if you'd even want to...."

"A transfer?"

He swore under his breath. "Rachel, I'm trying to ask you to marry me. To come to Houston with me."

"Then do."

It was that simple. That strange. That exciting.

"Marry me."

"Yes."

He stared at her as though she hadn't answered at all, and then burst into laughter, hugging her and kissing her. "I should have known you'd be able to simplify it. God...say it again."

"Yes. And yes, and yes."

He kissed her for all three, and then he added another long, draining kiss just because he said he needed the taste of her to get him through the next several hours, until they could be alone again in the privacy of a hotel room. Strangely enough, it made her stronger than she'd been feeling in hours.

He needed her...and she needed him. It was almost perfect.

A half hour later, with their suitcases in the trunk of the conservative FBI sedan, they said goodbye to Adorabella and Jewel.

Rachel kissed Adorabella on her withered, rose-scented cheek. "Would you like to host a wedding in a few days?" she whispered in the old woman's ear.

Years vanished from the old woman's face. "Something intimate but lively?"

"That will do."

"Oh, I'd love to. I'll talk to Jewel about something special for the punch."

"Do that," Rachel said, turning to her house-keeper.

They faced each other soberly. Slowly, dry smiles inched free on both of their mouths. "You know, you're not as scary as you think you are," she told her.

"Then I need to try harder...Doctor."

Rachel grinned and hugged her. "We'll talk again soon."

"I'll be here."

Joe escorted her into the back seat of the FBI car, and soon they were making their way up the driveway and turning onto the bridge. As she'd expected, the sun turned the sky apricot and tangerine.

She was so grateful for the second chance, the happiness she and Joe were being offered. So why was she dreading this crossing? No matter how hard she tried, she knew the moment they finished crossing the bridge, she would feel a part of herself lost forever.

She had to bite her lip as they approached *that* spot, clench her hands, but she couldn't resist looking out the window. She couldn't resist reaching out to touch the glass, and mouthing, "Goodbye."

A larger hand covered hers. Wonderfully warm, reassuringly confident. And a deep, smiling voice murmured, "Hey, Bright Eyes, it's okay. I'm here."

She spun around. Bright Eyes? *Bright Eyes?* Tears blinded her, but she knew where she was reaching.

Wrapping her arms around his neck, she whispered, "I know, Joe. Oh, God, I know."

* * * * *

The romantic suspense at

HARLEQUIN®

INTRIGUE

just got more intense!

On the precipice between imminent danger and
smoldering desire, they are

When your back is against the wall
and nothing makes sense, only one man
is strong enough to pull you from the brink—
and into his loving arms!
Look for all the books in this riveting new
promotion:

INTIMATE MOMENTS™

presents a riveting 12-book continuity series:

a Year of loving dangerously

Where passion rules and nothing is what it seems...

When dishonor threatens a top-secret agency, the brave
men and women of SPEAR are prepared to risk it all as they
put their lives—and their hearts—on the line.

Available February 2001:

SOMEONE TO WATCH OVER HER
by Margaret Watson

When SPEAR agent Marcus Waters discovered Jessica Burke on a
storm-swept beach, bruised, beautiful and in need of his protection,
he never imagined that sharing close quarters with her would lead
to spiraling passion. Or that this young beauty would entrust him
not only with her life—but with her innocence. Now, as they
waited out the danger together, the world-weary agent battled
an even greater enemy to his bachelor heart: love!

July 2000: MISSION: IRRESISTIBLE by Sharon Sala #1016
August: UNDERCOVER BRIDE by Kylie Brant #1022
September: NIGHT OF NO RETURN by Eileen Wilks #1028
October: HER SECRET WEAPON by Beverly Barton #1034
November: HERO AT LARGE by Robyn Amos #1040
December: STRANGERS WHEN WE MARRIED by Carla Cassidy #1046
January 2001: THE SPY WHO LOVED HIM by Merline Lovelace #1052
February: SOMEONE TO WATCH OVER HER by Margaret Watson #1058
March: THE ENEMY'S DAUGHTER by Linda Turner #1064
April: THE WAY WE WED by Pat Warren #1070
May: CINDERELLA'S SECRET AGENT by Ingrid Weaver #1076
June: FAMILIAR STRANGER by Sharon Sala #1082

*Available only from Silhouette Intimate Moments
at your favorite retail outlet.*

Where love comes alive™

HARLEQUIN®
INTRIGUE
opens the case files on:

TOP SECRET BABIES

Unwrap the mystery!

January 2001
#597 THE BODYGUARD'S BABY
Debra Webb

February 2001
#601 SAVING HIS SON
Rita Herron

March 2001
#605 THE HUNT FOR HAWKE'S DAUGHTER
Jean Barrett

April 2001
#609 UNDERCOVER BABY
Adrianne Lee

May 2001
#613 CONCEPTION COVER-UP
Karen Lawton Barrett

Follow the clues to your favorite retail outlet.

HARLEQUIN®
Makes any time special ™